POCO PANE, POCO VINO:
a little bread, a little wine

Stories and art by Gina Gigli
Recipes by Ruggero Gigli

POCO PANE, POCO VINO
a little bread, a little wine
Stories and art by Gina Gigli
Recipes by Ruggero Gigli

Book Design: Karen Hickson, Blue Sage Communications
Poem, page iv: Claudia Conlon
Some of the stories in this book have appeared in
slightly different form in *The Wine News* magazine.

Publisher's Cataloging-in-Publication
Gigli, Gina
Poco pane, poco vino : a little bread, a little wine / by Gina Gigli ;
with recipes by Ruggero Gigli. – 1st ed.

p. cm.
Includes bibliographical references and index.
ISBN: 0-9709082-0-2
1. Cookery, Italian. 2. Wine and wine making.
3. Intaglio printing. 4. Tuscany (Italy)—Description and
travel. 5. Sierra Nevada (Calif. and Nev.)—Description
and travel. I. Gigli, Ruggero. II. Title.

TX723.H53 2001   641.5945
QBI01-200260

Printed in the United States of America
by Whitmore Print and Imaging

Published by Villa Gigli Press
P.O. Box 307
Markleeville, California 96120
tel/fax: 530.694.2253
e-mail: ginagigli@gbis.com
www.villagigli.com

This book is written
in memory of our parents,
Lorenzo and Dina Gigli
and
Frank and Brownie Green.

We also wish to dedicate these pages to
our sons Ken, Andy and Patrick Hickson,
and especially our
daughter Dina Marina Gitelman,
daughter in law Karen Hickson and
friend Claudia Conlon
for their insightful editorial contributions,
and
friends Justin and Bonny Meyer for their support.

una foglia, molte foglie
one leaf, many leaves
silent truth beyond words

the green man filters, converts, releases
his dancers pause
spin gently to the tune of life
tiny vessels of wisdom
fading, freewheeling
grounded to the tune of death

green man
sustaining the breath you breathe
sustaining all the living world
endlessly

POCO PANE — A LITTLE BREAD

By Ian Harmer

Those who demand that Chef Ruggero Gigli should abide by the conventions of less intimate and interesting restaurants are likely to find themselves at the wrong end of one of his mock-wrath tirades, delivered with right index finger raised and pointing in the general direction of the nearest fast food eatery.

What Ruggero, his wife Gina and their cheerful helpers pull off every night that their Villa Gigli Trattoria is open for business is a miraculous blend of good food and wine, beautiful surroundings – mercifully miles away from the burger joints the chef smilingly derides – and casual comfort calculated to give customers the feeling that they're having dinner in a good friend's dining room. And dull old convention has nothing whatever to do with it.

Ruggero sometimes likes to pretend that he's an Italian-accented, Alpine County precursor of the New York "Soup Nazi" made famous in an episode of TV's *Seinfeld*. But the truth is that he's a warm-hearted, imaginative gourmet chef whose creations are unique even among other Italian restaurants.

Since Villa Gigli opened in Markleeville in 1992, Ruggero Gigli has been living a dream come true, and anyone choosing to play a role in that dream by making a reservation for dinner had better be ready for a unique and unforgettable experience.

In winter, dinner is served family-style inside the combined restaurant and art gallery that's the hub of Villa Gigli, with Gina's colorful artwork hanging on walls that tower above the intimately laid out dining area. Ruggero's wide open – and tiny – kitchen is just inside the entrance, and as his creations bubble and bake, he steps across the threshold from time to time to help Gina take care of his guests.

In summer – barring an occasional thunderstorm – the eating action moves out onto the restaurant's spacious deck, giving visitors the chance to marvel not just at the food but at some of the most beautiful surroundings to be enjoyed anywhere.

Markleeville was home to the Giglis long before they decided the time was right to stop dreaming about introducing Americans to the marvelous Italian dishes Ruggero's mother taught him how to cook way back in the 20th century, and actually do it.

Today, putting dozens of those wonderful recipes into a book so that Gigli devotees can prepare them in their own kitchens is not as brave or foolhardy a move as it might at first seem.

For a while, Ruggero – like any master of his art – was worried that he might be handing over priceless trade secrets, not so much to valued guests but to potential competitors.

But Gina was soon able to convince him that even if would-be trespassers into his unique territory were able to reproduce his dishes as colorfully and tastily as he does (unlikely!), they'd be missing one absolutely essential ingredient: Ruggero himself.

I read once that Desi Arnaz, the Cuban bandleader who was his wife's ever-exasperated straight man in TV's hit sitcom *I Love Lucy*, had a sign on his dressing-room door that warned: "English Broken Here!" and I have often thought of reproducing it as a gift for Ruggero's kitchen.

It's not that Ruggero is hard to understand – far from it – but his version of English is as unique and engaging as his interpretation of the traditional Italian dishes that flow from his kitchen.

At least a couple of times a night, he'll call his guests to order either to welcome them or to tell them a story that may or may not be connected with the food they have in front of them.

Ruggero does with words what he does with home-baked bread, homemade pasta and all the fresh, top quality ingredients that go into his inimitable dishes – he makes them his own.

What readers will find in the pages of this book is just a little taste of what Ruggero Gigli brought with him when he emigrated to the United States from Tuscany a few score years ago.

They can't have Ruggero himself with them in their kitchens, gesticulating excitedly, occasionally bursting into song and demonstrating that he enjoys his cooking every bit as much as his guests do.

Follow the recipes correctly, as any good cook does, and the results will be rewarding and satisfying – the best you can hope for if you're too far away to be able to spend an evening with Ruggero and Gina Gigli in their corner of a meadow in Markleeville.

Ian Harmer is a syndicated journalist and author who first wrote about Ruggero and Gina Gigli for the Reno Gazette-Journal in 1993 – and they have not been able to get rid of him since.

POCO VINO — A LITTLE WINE

By Justin Meyer

This book brings back vivid memories. Many were the times when Ruggero, Gina and I, and my wife Bonny got together at our house or theirs, and Ruggero made pasta and I poured my wine.

I met the Giglis soon after Bonny was doing a wine function for Silver Oak Cellars in conjunction with the Orange County Fair where she was a wine judge. She not only was our salesman in those early days of our winery, but also the mother of three, with our infant with her in a basket. She did not know the Giglis, but when she had to use the restroom she asked the people at the table next to her (Ruggero and Gina) if they'd watch her baby until she came back. They must have thought she was quite crazy to entrust her child to total strangers, but what were her options? Sometime later, I was introduced to the Giglis and it has been a fond friendship ever since.

I can remember one Easter in Markleeville, when Gina taught the two boys, who were then small, how to make intaglio prints, and they made designs for Easter. We still have them hanging on our wall. Gina has also been the instructor in art for our daughter Holly, and Holly has become quite good.

I still chide Ruggero when we are together by calling him a "dumb dago" and asking him why, after so many years in the U.S., can he still not speak English. We laugh, eat some more pasta and drink some more wine.

Villa Gigli has become a well-known pasta restaurant in the Sierra Nevada. My salesmen have wondered why I will go to Markleeville to do a Winemaker's Dinner for Ruggero, and I won't go to Chicago, New York or Dallas – very important markets. This is not about business. We have a great time.

I think you will have a great time with this book trying Ruggero's "homey" recipes. Let me say to you as you begin to experiment with Ruggero's recipes, *"Buon Appetito."*

Justin Meyer, founder and former winemaster of Silver Oak Cellars in Oakville, California, now is directing his enological knowledge toward wine consulting and his Meyer Family Port.

VINOUS IMPRESSIONS

By W.R. Tish

Excerpted from Wine Times, September/October 1990

Gina and Ruggero Gigli breathe life into the ancient art form of *intaglio* printing. The *intaglio* process is slow and painstakingly precise, so perhaps it is not surprising that the Giglis draw much of their artistic inspiration from wine, which undergoes a long, carefully tended journey from vine to glass. Just as winemakers coax nuances of flavor that set their work apart from other wines, the Giglis work in nuances of texture and color that distinguish their *intaglio* prints from such other visual media as watercolor or oil painting.

The artists' step-through process begins with Gina, whose images stem from hours spent in Napa Valley vineyards. "I have to go out there," she says. "I take a kind of shorthand – words, sketches, how I feel." She focuses her notes and drawings on evocative groupings of grape leaves, clusters, tendrils and vines; later, back home, she integrates the pieces into a rough composite whole. With this image as a guide, Gina then uses a needle-like steel instrument, called a Whistler's pen to scribe a zinc plate coated with a thin, protective layer of asphalt and beeswax.

After achieving an initial outline, she submerges the entire plate in a bath of nitric acid, which defines the barely incised lines. Proceeding to the aquatinting stage, Gina applies droplets of lacquer that resist the acid, so that ensuing acid baths can create the minute levels of depth in the zinc and ultimately create delicate gradations of tone and texture in the final print. After the plate is complete, Gina passes it to Ruggero for the inking stage. Following Gina's verbal instructions, Ruggero mixes dabs of special lithographic inks, like a painter blending oils on a palette. Then he places the inked plate face-down onto the paper. With one pauseless pull [through the press], Ruggero applies 2,000 pounds of consistent pressure, transferring the ink from the plate. After hanging a print to dry, Ruggero must carefully re-ink the plate; every print is an original.

Table of Contents

INTRODUCTION 2

Chapter 1 — WOMAN OF THE VINE 5

Chapter 2 — GODDESS OF GRAIN 13

Chapter 3 — GODDESS OF OLIVES 19

Chapter 4 — PROMISED LAND 25

Chapter 5 — EMPEROR'S LEGACY 35

Chapter 6 — KING'S BANQUET 51

Chapter 7 — SOLDIER OF FORTUNE 65

Chapter 8 — TWISTED TRYST 77

Chapter 9 — KEEPER OF THE LIGHT 87

Chapter 10 — EDIBLE LANDSCAPE 99

Chapter 11 — VIN SANTO TOSCANO 111

Chapter 12 — CHIANTI CLASSICO 121

Chapter 13 — FESTA al FRESCO 135

Chapter 14 — GREEN MAN 145

Chapter 15 — SWIRL AND SNIFF 157

Chapter 16 — HIDDEN WORKERS 171

PENSIERI — THOUGHTS 182

HISTORICAL FIGURES 183

FICTIONAL FIGURES 184

KITCHEN ITALIAN 185

RECIPE BOX 189

BOOK SHELF 192

INTRODUCTION

"Gina, I'm not going to open a restaurant! I just want to serve *poco pane, poco vino* – a little bread and a little wine – in our gallery on weekends." With those reassuring words, Ruggero convinced me that while he dabbled in the kitchen, I could putter in my art studio.

We had just returned home to Markleeville after a "sabbatical" of three years spent in Napa Valley's St. Helena. We each had freelanced for wineries from 1989 to 1992: Ruggero, by cooking Italian meals in vineyards, and I by etching wine-theme limited edition prints and engraving wine bottles.

With our move back to the mountains and our shared intention to slow down a bit, I was concerned that Ruggero would allow his idea of *poco pane, poco vino* to metamorphose into an Italian restaurant. And that's exactly what happened. Villa Gigli Trattoria was conceived and subsequently born in the art gallery right next to our house. Ruggero thrives by sharing his talent for cooking with those who travel the distance to enjoy a meal in our weekends-only restaurant. When guests ask how to pronounce our last name, I tell them "Jeel-yee" and that it means "lillies."

When he was a child in war-torn Italy, hunger had been Ruggero's constant companion. With his not-quite-perfect English, he explains, "You have a funny feeling in your stomach. It's always hungry, very empty feeling, and it make you feel nervous and yet full of energy. I saw people who had hunting dogs. They didn't feed the dogs for two or three days before they go hunting, so that the dogs were hungry, and they really hunt better because they are anxious to get the wild animals. My hunger, the most that satisfy it is *pane*. When I am nervous, I eat bread. Bread is comforting. It fills you up the stomach; then I guess if your stomach is full, you are happy. Because I grew up hungry and my stomach was empty, I was nervous and all excited. I was always looking for, like a hunting dog, food. It was a very simple bread that we ate, called *pane campagnolo* – country-style bread – and that's what I make every week in my *trattoria* in Markleeville."

Ruggero first apprenticed in a Tuscan country bakery at the tender age of 12, rising to become the head baker at the Forno Sartoni in the historic heart of Florence. Believing that "bread is the staff of life," he was drawn to the bakery's warm hearth.

Though well fed from the bread he ate and the "bread" he earned, at age twenty-six he began to experience other hunger pangs. Yearning for a different life with more opportunity, he emigrated to the United States and settled in Carson City, Nevada, where we met and eventually married. After remodeling or building various art studios and galleries in Nevada and in the California towns of Markleeville, Carmel and St. Helena, we have re-settled at Villa Gigli in Markleeville in the Sierra Nevada mountains. While Ruggero's *pane* and *pasta* evoke vivid memories of Tuscany, his sauces often evolve into variations of their original themes.

Ruggero explains, "I like to create my own compositions, just like Gina does with her paintings. Sometimes I design a recipe when I remember a place or an event, using products at hand and in season. Many of my recipes come from ancient times, others from early years in Italy and still more from recent years of life in California. I believe that the beauty of life is learning."

With his tiny kitchen open to the *trattoria* dining room, Ruggero, out of necessity, has developed a method of cooking he calls *al forno* – in the oven. After making the *pasta* in the morning, he then half-cooks it. "I drop the *pasta*, one sheet at a time, into boiling water in a large pot. When the water re-boils, I take the *pasta* out and put it on a clean white cloth to drain." After his sauces are completed, he cuts the *pasta* into various widths and assembles individual portions to be finished in the oven upon receiving orders in the evening. Baking ensures flavorful *salsa* and *pasta* that is tender yet *al dente* – not over-cooked.

When we visit Italy, not only do we love testing and tasting the bread and wine, but we also enjoy listening to stories about *poco pane, poco vino*. These "edible legends" may or may not be true, but they are fascinating and I have intertwined them with historical facts, sketches and *intaglio* prints from my studio, along with Ruggero's basic recipes and comments from his kitchen.

Civilization began
when mobile gatherers
became stabile farmers.

The oldest known cultivated crops,
GRAPES, GRAIN and OLIVES,
were harvested by hand and
crushed, ground and pressed by large millstones
powered by man, beast, water or wind.

As Siduri, Woman of the Vine and Maker of Wine, strolled in her garden by the edge of the sea, she saw a strange creature emerging from the shadows of the woods. As the apparition drew nearer, Siduri realized that the beast actually was a bearded and scruffy-looking man wrapped with animal skins. The wild man, known as Gilgamesh, had trekked endlessly through canyons and over mountain peaks in his search for the sea. At this stage in his journey, he had not come to the realization yet that his quest for the sea was less about catching a view of water than about discovering the meaning of life. As he stumbled out of the dark woods, he was amazed to see white-capped waves sparkling in the distance. Blinking in the bright sunlight, he made his way over a small sandy hill toward Siduri.

Immediately, he was struck motionless by the scene of Siduri's colorful garden, filled with trellised vines of emerald leaves and bronze tendrils, laden with lapis lazuli grapes and bordered by rows of golden grain. Siduri approached the man holding a bowl filled with ruby-red wine and a plate heaped with bread.

"Greetings, my name is Siduri. I would like you to accept wine from my vineyard and bread from my wheat field." Astonished by her offer, the wild man could only shuffle his bare feet and stare at her in silence. The Woman of the Vine and Maker of Wine tempted him with her soft voice, "Drink the wine, for it comes from the tree of life; eat the bread, for it is the staff of life."

Gilgamesh gratefully quenched his thirst with seven bowls of wine and quelled his hunger with a loaf of bread. After satisfying his thirst and hunger and once more gazing at the lovely vineyard, he concluded that his unkempt appearance was inappropriate. He washed in the sea, anointed his body with olive oil, groomed his matted hair and dressed in clean clothing provided by his hostess.

Over the years, as Gilgamesh continued his pilgrimage, he always remembered the Woman of the Vine, who not only cultivated a vineyard from wilderness but also civilized a man from the wild.

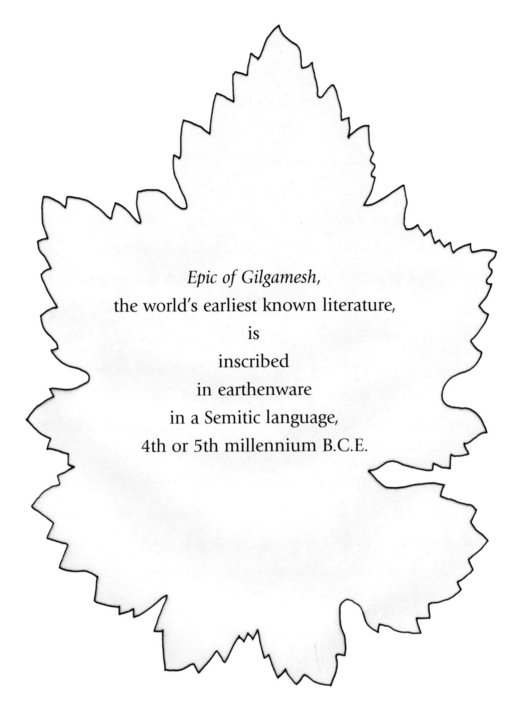

Epic of Gilgamesh,
the world's earliest known literature,
is
inscribed
in earthenware
in a Semitic language,
4th or 5th millennium B.C.E.

In 1991, when we lived in St. Helena in the Napa Valley, I was invited to the Robert Mondavi Winery to a symposium about recent findings of the origins and ancient history of wine. The main attraction was a reconstructed Persian amphora, billed as "The World's Earliest Known Wine Jar."

I learned that the sands of time had been shifted to a new level in the 1990s by the perseverance of a dedicated graduate student of Near-Eastern Studies at the University of Toronto, Canada, who also proved that not all of the great archaeological discoveries happen at the dig. When Virginia Badler found some ancient shards in a museum drawer at the University and pieced them into an amphora of incredible beauty, she initiated a process that ultimately restored a gap in the chronology of winemaking. The lost time represented a lag of 500 years – from the Bronze to the Neolithic Age. These clay fragments, along with many other artifacts carbon-dated to the fourth century B.C.E., had been excavated by a team of Royal Ontario Museum archaeologists in 1973 in the Zagros Mountains of Iran at a site known as Godin Tepe.

As sunshine filtered through the glass-paneled roof of the winery's conference room onto the venerable vessel, Badler described her odyssey. After gluing the shards together and wondering about the reddish stain inside the vessel, she asked various authorities if the color possibly could be attributed to wine residue. She was told no, that the red hue must have been some kind of paint or glaze used by the ancient potter, since viticulture was not known to have existed then. She questioned the significance of the raised band-rope design applied in two inverted "U" shapes along opposite exterior sides. Rope patterns usually suggest the placement of real ropes, so she speculated that the jar had been designed to lie on its side and that the ropes might have formed the world's earliest wine rack. Badler persisted with her ever-growing conviction that the amphora had been a wine container. There were other artifacts from the same discovery area: a funnel, which she had pieced together first; unfired clay stoppers; beveled-rim bowls. She continued to perceive the archaeological site as a winemaking shop and imagined that the funnel would have filtered grape juice into the amphora; the stoppers would have sealed wine jugs; the bowls would have been the equivalent of wineglasses.

Ultimately caught up with Badler's visualizations, other scientists were swept into the vortex of the mystery surrounding this Pre-Bronze Age vessel. The chemical confirmation that wine actually had been inside the 3,500 B.C.E. jar came from Dr. Patrick E. McGovern, a research scientist at the University of Pennsylvania, by means of a simple test using infrared spectroscopic analysis. He told the audience that he had boiled the shards with acetone to extract a small amount of deposit and then determined the residue to be tartaric acid. He also tested residue from a "known" wine jar dated fifth century from the opposite end of the "Fertile Crescent" – the site of Gebel Adda in southern Egypt – using the same methodology. The similar chemical evidence accompanied by the knowledge that tartaric acid is found in nature almost exclusively in grapes, plus the archaeological evidence, proved the existence of wine in the Godin Tepe vessel. McGovern concluded that this ". . . has important implications for the beginnings of civilization and viticulture in the Near East."

Ancient amphorae not only contained wine, but also olive oil, grain and fish. Dr. Louis Grivetti, University of California at Davis expert on ancient nutrition, said that the fermented fish product stored in amphorae was called garum. Dr. Francoise Formenti from the University of Lyon, France, added, "Amphorae were the common containers that ancient people used to transport liquid or solid food products. They were usually considered to be non-returnable jars – the same as the plastic bottles of today." British paleobotanist Dr. Jane Renfrew said that ancient potters shaped their earthenware wine jars on grape leaves, which left impressions of wild grape leaves fired into the bottoms of the amphorae.

"The earliest grapes were wild," said Dr. Solomon Katz, University of Pennsylvania biological anthropologist, going on to explain that animal skins and pouches were used for gathering and transporting food stuffs that had been hunted. The gatherers likely would have picked the ripest and sweetest grapes on the vines. Since natural yeasts bloomed on the grape skins, the sugar was converted to alcohol as the grapes were crushed by their own weight in the skin bags. The discovery of seeds and the clear emergence of agriculture brought about great economic and social changes 5,000 years ago. The dawn of civilization glimmered when humans consciously set out to cultivate by vegetatively propagating, waiting five to seven years for the crops to mature. Dr. Katz concluded, "Wine was probably one of the earliest fermented foods and of great importance in the development of human culture. Wine was not used for its alcoholic properties, but for the social aspects. Wine is the counterbalance in socialization."

Many health researchers agree that a glass or two of wine a day may indeed "keep the doctor away." Moderate consumption of wine can inhibit arteriosclerosis, heart attack and common stroke. Quercitin, an antioxidant, also found in grapeskins, is an effective anti-cancer agent.

PREHISTORIC WINE

Leather bag
Sweet wild grapes
Natural yeasts

Gather sweet wild grapes and stuff them into an animal-skin pouch slung over shoulder. Continue picking grapes, making certain to choose the ripest, juiciest berries on the vine. When the bag is full of sweet grapes, walk back to the cave. Allow the bag and grapes to remain outside in the sun until fermentation is complete. Invite other cave dwellers to your party.

Key
for
Ingredient Consistency
for
POCO PANE, POCO VINO Recipes:

Salt – Sea, Coarsely Ground
Pepper – Black, Coarsely Ground
Flour – Unbleached
Olive Oil – Extra Virgin
Onions – Red
Vinegar – Red Wine
Canned Tomatoes – Crushed, Non-Seasoned
Jack Cheese – Dry Monterey
Butter – Unsalted
Eggs – Jumbo

With her long hair blowing in the soft breeze, Greek goddess Demeter strolled through the meadow, smiling to see all of the nourishing grasses ripening with grain. As Earth Mother, she was not only watching over the crops to ensure their bountiful continuity but also over her young daughter, Persephone. Delighted to see a lovely narcissus sprouting from the grass, Persephone bent down and picked it. Immediately, the earth opened and she was plunged into the depths of the underworld whereupon hateful Hades claimed her as his bride.

Furious with Hades and in retaliation for the kidnapping, distraught Demeter immediately withdrew the generous offerings of purple grapes, golden grain and silvery olive trees she had given the world. Shouting a powerful curse, she caused grapevines to die, wheat to shrivel and olive leaves to drop to the ground.

Deprived of their grapes, grain and olives, everyone became angry as starvation seeped through the land. Alarmed by this desperate situation, mighty god Zeus sent his messenger Hermes to the underworld to demand that Hades send Persephone back to Demeter. Shaken by Zeus's strong edict, Hades agreed. But just at the moment of Persephone's departure from the dark depths, Hades offered her a pomegranate. The girl made the terrible mistake of eating one pomegranate seed, thereby sealing her fate. Eating anything in the underworld guaranteed imprisonment through eternity.

Zeus struck the best bargain possible with Hades. The two agreed that Persephone would endure the oppressive darkness of the underworld for three months each year, but Hades would allow her to bask in the sunshine of the real world the other nine months.

In this way, the seasons have come to be marked by the energy of Demeter's mood swings. When she is mourning her daughter's descent into the underworld, the earth becomes cold and barren. When her daughter returns each spring, Demeter joyously encourages young shoots of grapevines, grain and olive trees to swell, bloom in summer and ripen in autumn.

"See in the mind's eye
wind blowing chaff on ancient threshing
floors
when men with fans toss up the trodden
sheaves, and yellow-haired Demeter,
puff by puff,
divides the chaff and grain."

From Homer's epic poem, The Iliad,

oldest surviving text in Greek literature,

8th century B.C.E.

When primitive people realized that grains gathered from grasses could be eaten either as bread or as porridge, they began to group together and settle down to plant crops. Civilization began when hunters stopped gathering wild grains and actually planted and harvested barley and wheat in the "Fertile Crescent" river valleys of the Tigris and Euphrates. Flat cakes were made by adding some water to grain and cooking the mixture on hot rocks. By adding more water proportionally to the amount of grain, they also created a thin gruel.

Which came first – bread or wine? Since wild yeast cells grow naturally on both grain and grapes, a relatively parallel history could be surmised. However, bread without leavening was the only type of bread baked until the Egyptians "discovered" the benefits of yeast. Who really knows? Perhaps a slave accidentally splashed fermented wine into a baker's flat bread dough and then watched in amazement as his bread puffed up.

Leavening legends abound, perhaps told to apprentice bakers as a form of initiation. One story claims that bread yeast originated from cow dung. Another ridiculous tale involved bakers treading dough in huge bread vats and producing yeast from the fungi living between their toes. Infinitely more appetizing is the premise that dormant yeast spores float sleepily around in the air, waking up to integrate with gooey dough. Starches and sugars are metabolized, giving off gases (alcohol and carbon dioxide) that expand the dough.

Laborers who were building the pyramids of Egypt evidently thought that these raised breads were superior to the old sun-baked patty cakes and accepted bread as their salary. Today's slang phrase "I earn enough bread" could have been uttered 6,000 years ago.

Roman artisans were so proud of their individual bread creations that they stamped their names into loaves, and the bakery became not only a place to buy bread products but also a fashionable place to meet and greet friends, just as it is now.

As an important member of the Mediterranean Trio, grain is praised by nutritionists for providing necessary fiber in the diet and playing a big role in countering high cholesterol.

PREHISTORIC BREAD

Handfuls of grain

Sun-warmed rock

Some water

Mix grain with water. Divide dough into fist-sized portions and smash each one into a flat patty. Leave patties on a large, warm rock to "bake" in the sun while you are hunting. Upon return to cave, serve "bread" with fire-roasted game. If hunting was unsuccessful, just eat the "bread."

Athena, Greek goddess of wisdom, and Poseidon, Greek god of the sea, quarreled about naming a new city in the province of Attica. Zeus, powerful ruler of the gods, decided to act as mediator of their dispute and declared, "The best way to determine the winner is to hold a contest."

Although intelligent Athena was highly regarded by the citizens for her talents in agriculture and art, many of the people were impressed by Poseidon's dramatic ability to turn his temper tantrums into fearsome earthquakes sending fractured rocks splashing into the sea.

After Zeus laid down the rules, "Whoever conjures up the most useful gift for the benefit of humanity will win," the citizens swarmed up the Acropolis hill on a very hot summer day to watch the spectacle of two deities trying to outwit each other.

Poseidon confidently strode into the center of the crowd. With sweat glistening on his brow, he yelled loudly, "Watch this!" In a mighty demonstration of power, he thrust his trusty trident down into the ground. Instantly, a magnificent horse sprang forth from the earth, and the people shouted their approval for his magical sleight of hand.

Smiling serenely, gray-eyed Athena then took her stance in the circle of jurors. She gracefully whirled around and skillfully struck her sword straight into the earth. A mature olive tree sprouted from the ground, its silvery leaves shading the oh-so-silent crowd.

Athena calmly explained, "This olive tree not only will provide shade from the sun in the summer and wood for fires in the winter, but most importantly, the oil from the fruit will provide humanity with many benefits: illumination, heat, cooking oil, lubrication, moisturizing." Athena continued to praise the attributes of olives for food, adding, "Olive oil also will be used as food for the soul in ceremonial rituals."

Upon learning about the virtues of olives, the audience broke into cheers, unanimously voting Athena the winner. She named the new city "Athens" and taught the citizens how to cultivate olive trees and produce olive oil.

The poet Homer described olive oil
as "Liquid Gold."

In his epic, *The Odyssey*,
8th century, B.C.E., he wrote,
"And bright-eyed Athena
sent them a favorable wind,
a strong-blowing west wind
that sang over
the wine-dark sea."

At the end of forty days of flood throughout the land, Noah opened a porthole he had made in his ark and sent one dove aloft to determine if the waters were receding from the earth. The bird circled the world but returned to the ark, since water was still covering the land. Noah put out his hand, grasped the dove and brought him back into the ark. After waiting seven more days, he sent the dove forth once again. That evening, when the dove returned with a new olive sprig in its beak, Noah was joyful in the realization that the waters had receded finally. This Biblical story symbolizes the promise of life, and the image of the dove, olive branch in beak, represents peace.

Tracing the genealogy of the olive tree through time, its main trunk could be found on the eastern shores of the Mediterranean around 6,000 years ago. However, its roots extended far back into prehistory to the stony soils of Asia Minor.

Phoenicians spread olive culture to Spain and Greece around 1700 B.C.E., and the Greeks subsequently transported olives to Italy. Ancient Mediterranean people used olives, and especially olive oil, as nourishment, illumination, ritual anointing, moisturizer and even as an emollient to smooth "troubled waters" when fishing. Ancient olive oil was transported in amphorae, and amazingly, some of these clay jars were stamped in *sgrafitto* – incised design – stating the owner's name, location of the olive grove, name of trader and amount of taxes due for the oil.

Wreaths of olive leaves were first given as prizes to the victors of the original Greek Olympic Games in Olympia in 752 B.C.E., according to the Roman chronicle Phlegon.

Olive oil, the third member of the Mediterranean Trio, is a monounsaturated fat that stimulates metabolism and promotes digestion, is a good source of antioxidants and is believed to help retard the effects of aging.

PREHISTORIC OLIVE OIL

Ripe olives

Large stones

Grass

Pick ripe olives. Crush olives into mash with stone. Pat grass into mat on large stone. Spread mash over mat. Pat another mat to cover mash. Press with large stone, separating water from oil. Pour oil over sun-baked bread. Accompany with fermented grape juice.

Pinot Noir

Moses sent a reconnaissance team to explore the land of Canaan. When the men returned from their trip, they rushed over to Moses to report their discoveries in the Promised Land. They may have asked Moses, "Which would you like to hear first, the bad news or the good news?" Evidently Moses chose the good news, because the leader of the expedition enthusiastically described the lay of the land of Canaan: "It was the season of early grapes when we went into the land to which you sent us. The rivers flowed with milk and honey, and the trees bloomed with flowers and fruit. In the Valley of Eschol we lopped off a vine branch with clusters of grapes so huge that we had to carry them on a pole over our shoulders all the way back. We also lugged back luscious figs and juicy pomegranates for everyone's enjoyment."

Moses commented that the land indeed sounded promising, but demanded to know the bad news.

The leader of the exploration team shuddered as he remembered the frightening encounter in Canaan (paraphrased from the Old Testament, Numbers 13: 21-28): "The down side is that the land is inhabited by terrible giants, who made us feel as insignificant and helpless as tiny grasshoppers. We could have been trampled under the boots of those mammoth men, and then we would not have lived to bring you the fruits of our journey."

More tempting words about the Promised Land are from the eighth chapter of Deuteronomy, "But Yahweh your God is bringing you into a prosperous land, a land of streams and springs, of waters that well up from the deep in valleys and hills, a land of wheat and barley, of vines and figs, of pomegranates, a land of olives, of oil, of honey, a land where you will eat bread without stint, where you will want nothing, a land where the stones are of iron, where the hills may be quarried for copper. You will eat and have all you want, and you will bless Yahweh your God in the rich land he has given you."

When people strive to reach elusive Promised Lands, it seems that they have always found both good and bad awaiting them.

"Each man
will sit
under his
vine and fig tree
with no one
to trouble him."

Old Testament,

Micah 4:4

We all have visions of a "Promised Land." For many, it represents a spiritual after-life for the soul. It also may signify a better place to live in the here-and-now. In Ruggero's words, "Going to the 'Promised Land of America' became my dream. I plotted and planned how I could get there."

Though World War II cut Ruggero's education short in the 4th grade, he continued to be hungry for knowledge. It was customary in the Valle del Mugello for sons to follow their fathers into family businesses, but since his father had died near the end of the war, Ruggero would not become a produce salesman like Lorenzo Gigli. Determined to succeed on his own, Ruggero took his first steps in the direction of America by becoming a baker's apprentice in Borgo San Lorenzo and later moved to Firenze where he worked in the famous Forno Sartoni until he was 26.

"One scheme I dreamed up was to walk to Russia and then row in a little boat across the Bering Straight. To me, America was the land of freedom and opportunity, a land full of people with ideas and determination. I felt that God had given me two gifts – determination and the ability to work hard. I arrived in America in 1959, not by rowboat from Russia to Alaska, but on a Pan American jet from Rome to New York with money I had saved by working overtime in the bakery."

 Ruggero does thank God for the opportunities he has been given in America. He says, "Fortunately, I've had the strength to work hard. I really like to work because it gives me pleasure to stay healthy physically and mentally."

Ruggero has organized some of his recipes involving milk, honey, grapes and figs into a menu to honor the Biblical "Promised Land." When asked about pomegranates, he replied, "Forget about pomegranates; they're too messy."

BIBLICAL MENU
· · · · · · · · · · · · · ·

INSALATA di CUORI di PALME
PALM HEART SALAD

FILETTO con FICHI
FILET with FIG SAUCE

MIGLIACCIOLE
DESSERT PANCAKES

INSALATA di CUORI di PALME

PALM HEART SALAD

8 servings

2 cups small white dried beans

8 cups water

> Soak beans in water 12 hours to cover, rinsing twice.

6 tablespoons olive oil

2 tablespoons red wine vinegar

4 leaves fresh sage

8 garlic cloves, chopped coarsely

1 teaspoon coarsely ground pepper

> Simmer, uncovered, for 1 hour. Skim off foam; drain beans; cool; refrigerate.

1 head butter lettuce

1 head *radicchio* – chicory

> Separate leaves of lettuces; rinse and dry well. Place leaves in radiating circular patterns on 8 salad plates, alternating the pale green leaves of the butter lettuce with those of the red *radicchio*.

1 can (14-ounce) hearts of palm, refrigerated for 3 hours

8 basil sprigs – tips only – with 4 or 5 leaves on each tip

> Cut palm hearts <u>diagonally</u> in 1/2-inch slices and arrange over lettuce leaves. Mound a *duomo* – dome – of beans in the center of the radiating leaves and palm hearts. Stick a sprig of *basilico* – basil – into the top of each *duomo*.

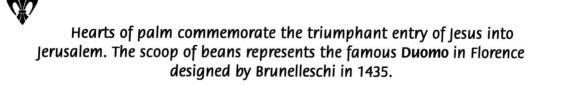

Hearts of palm commemorate the triumphant entry of Jesus into Jerusalem. The scoop of beans represents the famous Duomo in Florence designed by Brunelleschi in 1435.

FILETTO con FICHI

FILET with FIG SAUCE

8 servings

SALSA al FICO – FIG SAUCE

8 fresh black figs – or 12 dried black figs, chopped finely

1/2 cup pine nuts, chopped finely

4 cloves, chopped finely

1/2 lb. unsalted butter

1/2 cup Amaretto

1 cup Sauvignon Blanc

> Stir ingredients together in the top of a *bagnomaria* – double boiler – and simmer over hot water for 30 minutes.

8 steak filets, all fat trimmed off

> Grill steaks over very hot fire 3 minutes each side for medium-rare. Place each filet on a warmed plate and pour hot *Salsa al Fico* over.

This sauce came about when Gina and I lived in Napa Valley, and some good friends who had beautiful fig trees on their property gave us a bucket of ripe black figs. I figured I had to do something with all of those figs. The two of us certainly couldn't eat them all. I had been asked by Sterling Vineyards to cater a lunch for 60 people in the vineyards, so I created a larger version of this sauce and poured it over 60 steaks. Filetto con Fichi has since become the favorite *speciale* on our Villa Gigli menu.

MIGLIACCIOLE

DESSERT PANCAKES

8 servings

2 cups unbleached flour

4 cups tepid water

2 tablespoons olive oil

Stir water into flour with a wooden spoon, and then beat the batter with a wire whip. Drop batter by the tablespoon into very hot, but not smoking, olive oil in a skillet. Cook each pancake one minute on each side and, with a spatula, remove to a serving plate lined with paper towels. Keep pancakes hot by placing the serving plate into a 300-degree oven until ready to serve.

1 cup wildflower honey

Drizzle warmed honey over each pancake.

I like honey because ancient people used it. Honey was around before anyone tried to grow a crop. So this recipe is basic and also the most economical **Migliacciole** that I make. I make it without eggs because when my daughter was a kid, she would beg me to make **Migliacciole**. Up here in the mountains we always keep flour and honey on hand, but sometimes I would look into my refrigerator and not find any eggs. Since I didn't want to disappoint her, I would make the pancakes anyway, and she has never known the difference; not until she reads this book.

SALVIA, RAMERINO and BASILICO –
SAGE, ROSEMARY and BASIL –
are the favorite herbs
of Tuscany.
When sage is growing,
it imparts a magical aroma and velvet
touch and is used to season lamb, poultry, pork and game.
Its name comes from the Latin word *salvere* – to cure.
Keeping company with tomatoes,
basil perks up salads
and is mashed into fresh green *pesto*.
Remember rosemary for sautéeing
and for the perfume and flavor it adds
to many sauces.

Roman Wine Cup
1st Century A.D.

Marcus watched in horror as Roman soldiers unceremoniously dumped sack after sack of grain into the Tiber River. "Stop!" he shouted to the men as he broke from the crowd and ran down to the dock, "Why are you doing this? Can't you see how skinny we all are? We're almost to the point of starvation, and you're tossing this grain into the river?"

"Stand back and get out of our way before we throw you bags-of-bones into the river, too!" the captain threatened, "We have our orders from the Emperor. This flour is moldy and bug-infested. It's unfit for dogs to eat."

Despotic Imperatore Nerone had issued the edict to get rid of the stored creepy, crawly grain. Though attempting to follow the tradition of previous rulers by feeding the masses *Panem et Circenses* – bread for filling up stomachs and circuses to distract the starving – Nerone was hampered by the inability to keep insects from infesting stored grain. This politician wasn't giving bread away from the goodness of his heart but was instituting his brand of crowd control by giving a few "crumbs to the bums."

Marcus stomped back to the crowd and yelled, "We must find a way to preserve flour! The granaries are humid and damp, and our bread turns moldy and riddled with insects. Even though the emperor imports amphorae of wheat on ships from Egypt to supply our huge city, the bugs feast before we do."

Torinus responded to his friend's demand. "Marcus, when I lived in another section of the city, I watched women working wheat flour into dough. Rather than shape the dough into bread loaves for baking, they rolled out thin sheets that were then dried in the sun. I've heard that those flat dry pieces called *lagane* – noodles – are safe to keep for over a year. The women make *lagane* as soon as they get the flour, before the bugs can burrow in."

Marcus shouted, "By Jove, you've got it! Our wives can make *lagane*, too. Let's go to the circus and celebrate the noodle solution by betting on tonight's chariot race."

The world's oldest recorded cookbook,

De Re Coquinaria – About Cookery,

handed down through the ages,

was written by

gastronome M. Gabius Apicius of Imperial Rome

in the first century.

Sketchy descriptions of *lagane* and *pultes*

were the forerunners of *lasagne* and *polenta.*

When Nero became emperor at the age of 17 and was still under the guidance of his tutors, he displayed interest and compassion for the Roman citizens. Later on during his rule, the sludge of his egocentric, cruel and immoral behavior seeped through the structure of Imperial Rome, permeating every faction. After a large portion of Rome burned to the ground in the year 64, and Nero turned away from the crisis with indifference, his response became the classic metaphor for denial: "While Rome burned, Nero fiddled."

When anguish over real or imagined pain is ignored, watch out for backlash. Nero appeared on stage to sing his new *opera* just days after the city's conflagration. Many of the million or so Roman citizens had been displaced, burned or killed by the raging fire. Angered by the emperor's uncaring attitude toward their suffering, their anger turned to blame. In response, Nero pointed his finger at the Christians, initiating the terrible persecution in the arena where Christ's followers were tortured and tossed to savage animals. For many people the circus had ceased to be entertaining.

Though large Roman ships transported grain, wine and oil in amphorae from Egypt and other foreign ports, hunger continued to haunt the populace. Grain was the only salvation for the urban poor, who survived by making noodles with flour and water. *Pasta* is known to have pre-dated Roman times, as evidenced by an Etruscan tomb from the 4th century B.C.E. embellished with relief depictions of pasta tools. Marco Polo may have brought rice noodles back to Italy from his travels to Asia, but this was not the first *pasta* seen by his *paesani*.

From Roman times on, Italian city dwellers have eaten water-based dried pasta. Only the wealthy enjoyed fresh and tasty *tagliatelle* – noodles made with eggs. Country folk, who kept chickens in their yards, have always had an abundant egg supply and egg-rich *tagliatelle*.

LAGANE

DRIED NOODLES
8 servings

2 cups spelt (wheat flour)

1 cup water

Marcus's wife heaped the flour on a table and made a hole in the center of the flour. She slowly added water and kneaded the mass into a ball of dough. When the water and flour were mixed well, she rolled out the dough with a pole and made the dough as thin as possible. She added extra flour as needed to keep the dough from sticking to her hands or to the table. She cut the thin dough into strips and put them on a linen cloth and found a safe place on the roof to dry her *lagane*. Whenever Nero and his soldiers doled out flour to the neighborhood, Marcus's wife and the other women dutifully made *lagane* while the men gleefully partied at the circus.

This recipe for Lagane comes mostly from my imagination. It's the way that I think the ancient Romans made their dried pasta, though I never make pasta without eggs. Since we eat the pasta the same day I make it, I rarely dry it.

TAGLIATURA - NOODLE CUTTING TECHNIQUE

The *Tagliatelle* recipe (page 41) is basic for Ruggero's *pasta*.

Taglierini – 1/8-inch-wide by 8-inches-long

Tagliatelle – 1/2-inch-wide by 8-inches-long

Taglieroni – 1-inch-wide by 12-inches-long

For the three types of pasta above, Ruggero forms the dough into a 3-inch-diameter roll and then slices it with a sharp knife.

Cannelloni – 4-inches wide by 14-inches-long

Lasagne – 9-inches-wide by 13-inches-long

Tortellini – 4-inch squares

Ruggero slices these three types of *pasta* from the flat sheets of dough.

TAGLIATELLE

BASIC NOODLES

8 servings

2 cups unbleached flour

4 medium-sized fresh eggs

Heap the flour on counter. With the bottom of measuring cup, form a crater in the flour, so that it looks like a *vulcano* – volcano. Break eggs into the *vulcano* and slowly incorporate the flour into the eggs, from the center outward, using both hands. Mix the dough very well with hands and form it into a ball. Roll out the dough with a rolling pin or double-roller *pasta* machine. Do not use an extruding machine. Stretch the dough as thin as possible, sprinkling a little flour over the dough, roller and counter as needed to prevent the dough from sticking. Cut and arrange *Tagliatelle* on a clean white cloth. Put a large pot of water to boil with a couple of tablespoons of olive oil and drop *Tagliatelle* into it. Keep stirring, and when the water re-boils, drain *Tagliatelle* in a large strainer and serve immediately with sauce.

Mamma rolled out **Tagliatelle** every day for the noontime meal. She usually made **Pomarola Sauce** to go with it. Mamma always said, "Start the water to boil for Tagliatelle just as you start cooking the pomorola." By the time the sauce was finished, the **pasta** was cooked. That was our lunch – pasta, pane and a little vino! Parmigiano, on top of the grater, was passed around. I make **Tagliatelle** with exactly the same ingredients that Mamma used – flour and eggs and scrubbed-clean hands. If I'm making **Tagliatelle** for friends in their house, and they don't have a rolling pin, I use their clean broom handle. In my house I roll the dough through my hand-turned pasta machine, and in my **trattoria** I use my electric dough-thinning machine.

ROMAN MENU
· · · · · · · · · · · · · ·

GUSTUM VERSATILE

MOVEABLE APPETIZERS

Crostini al Fegatini – Little Toasts with Liver Spread

Uova alla Diavola – Deviled Eggs

HERBAE RUSTICA

FIELD HERBS

Insalata Mista – Mixed Green Salad

ASSATURAM SIMPLICEM

SIMPLE ROAST

Maiale al Miele – Honey-Glazed Pork Roast

PISAM SIVE FABAM VITELLIAN

PEAS in-the-style-of VITELLIUS

Piselli con Porri – Peas with Leeks

PATINA VERSATILIS VICE DULCIS

PINE NUT CUSTARD

Latte Imperiale – Imperial Custard

For a special dinner in our trattoria in 1994, Ruggero was guided by recipes from Apicius's De Re Coquinaria – About Cookery. Since most of the directions have been written and translated in different languages over many years and only list the ingredients, Ruggero has improvised with his own methods. Though grain was the most important staple in the Roman diet, Apicius didn't include recipes for bread, so Ruggero made his Pane Campagnolo.

CROSTINI al FEGATINI

TOASTS with LIVER SPREAD

8 servings

4 tablespoons olive oil

2 small leaves sage, finely chopped

1 pound chicken livers, fat cut off, each cut in half, washed and dried

> In a skillet, bring olive oil to a hot point, but not smoking. Add sage, and drop *Fegatini* – little livers – into hot, sage-infused oil. Sauté for 5 minutes, turning them frequently. Remove livers from pan.

2 tablespoons capers

2 tablespoons vinegar

4 cloves garlic, chopped finely

Juice of 1 lemon

Dash of salt and pepper

> Chop all ingredients together and then purée in a blender.

5 thin slices *Pane Campagnolo* (page 58), cut in 2-inch squares lightly toasted, or 16 thin slices sourdough baguette, lightly toasted.

> Spread *Fegatini* mixture over toasts.

Crostini al Fegatini is one of my preferred antipasti. Mamma used to make it for special occasions when I was a kid – and then I never had enough. This was the first recipe I "stole" from my mother. I am saying "stole" because she never would tell me how she made it, so I just watched her out of the corner of my eye.

UOVA alla DIAVOLA

DEVILED EGGS

8 servings

8 medium-sized eggs

1 teaspoon salt

1 tablespoon vinegar

> Put eggs in a big pan; cover them with cold water with the salt and vinegar. Bring the water to a boil; lower the temperature immediately and let the eggs simmer slowly for 20 minutes. Run cold water over eggs and gently tap the shells to make a crackle pattern. Peel shells. Cut each egg in half lengthwise. Transfer yolk into a bowl and mash with a fork.

3 teaspoons mayonnaise

2 teaspoons capers

2 teaspoons anchovy paste

Juice of 1/2 lemon

Finely chopped peel of 1/2 lemon

2 teaspoons white wine

4 teaspoons fresh basil, chopped coarsely

> Mix all of these ingredients together and stir into mashed egg yolks. Spoon mixture into the 16 egg-white halves.

 *I enjoy fixing **Uova alla Diavola** at the last minute when I don't have too much time because I always have these ingredients on hand. I've learned that Americans enjoy deviled eggs and feel festive since they associate these eggs with parties and picnics. Of course, mine are different. So they get a shock when they first taste them, but on second taste, they like them.*

INSALATA MISTA

MIXED GREEN SALAD

8 servings

8 handfuls mixed tender, young salad greens

A few red *radicchio* leaves

A few basil leaves

> Wash the leaves very well; put them in the center of a large clean, white dish towel; draw up the corners; take outside and <u>vigorously</u> swing the bundle three times by your side to shake out any moisture. Tear the larger leaves in half and put the well-dried leaves into a large salad bowl.

4 garlic cloves, chopped coarsely

1/4 onion, sliced in strips

16 Mediterranean-style olives, chopped (pits removed)

> Mix into salad.

1/4 cup olive oil

Spritz vinegar

Dash salt

2 dashes pepper

> Gently mix olive oil and very little vinegar, a little salt and generous amount of pepper into salad.

2 tablespoons honey-roasted sunflower seeds

Some herb or edible flowers (lavender, sage, nasturtiums, violas)

> Divide into 8 small salad plates and sprinkle seeds and flowers over.

> *Some people think that my Insalata Mista is for "Yuppies," but on the contrary – this salad goes way back to the Roman times, as described by Apicius, who definitely wasn't a "Yuppie."*

MAIALE al MIELE

HONEY-GLAZED PORK ROAST
8 servings

MAIALE – PORK

4-pound pork loin roast, with ALL fat and skin trimmed off

1/2 cup olive oil

> "Close" the *maiale* by searing it on all sides in hot olive oil in covered roasting pan in 400-degree oven. Remove *maiale* from pan in order to use the same pan to cook *Buon Battuto*.

MARINATURA – MARINADE

1/2 cup olive oil

2 teaspoons Worcestershire sauce

2 teaspoons chopped garlic

1 teaspoon pepper

> Mix ingredients together and marinate *maiale* – pork – for two hours, turning it every 30 minutes.

BUON BATTUTO – GOOD CHOPPED MIXTURE (page 48)

> After *Buon Battuto* is finished, add *maiale* to *battuto* in roasting pan, cover and roast 1 hour.

MIELE — HONEY

1/4 cup honey

> Take pan out of oven and drizzle honey over *maiale*. Roast, uncovered, for 30 more minutes. Remove *maiale* from pan; cool for 20 minutes before cutting into 1/2-inch-thick slices. Arrange slices on 8 warmed plates and pour the warm sauce from the roasting pan over each slice.

In the old Roman days before sugar came
along,

honey was often used

to give a touch of sweetness to meats.

When Ruggero visited Pompeii,

he saw an interesting motto.

An innkeeper had inscribed on his wall,

"Ubi perna cocta est si conive apponitur
non gustat pernam
linguit ollam aut caccabum –

My guests will lick the saucepan that
cooked this ham."

SOFFRITTO

SAUTÉ

8 servings

1/4 cup olive oil

1/2 onion, chopped coarsely

8 garlic cloves, chopped coarsely

> Slowly and lightly sauté onions in olive oil for 7 minutes. Add garlic and turn off heat, stirring for 3 minutes.

BUON BATTUTO

GOOD CHOPPED MIXTURE

8 servings

1/2 cup olive oil

1/2 onion, chopped coarsely

2 medium-sized carrots, cut in chunks

2 stalks celery, cut in chunks

8 garlic cloves, chopped coarsely

2 teaspoons fresh rosemary, chopped finely

1/2 cup parsley, chopped coarsely

> Sauté onion slowly for 7 minutes in olive oil and then add remaining ingredients and sauté slowly, stirring every few minutes, for an additional 15 minutes.

> *When I was growing up, Mamma made Buon Battuto almost every day. The kitchen smelled so good while Mamma chopped and sautéed those good vegetables. Buon Battuto is the foundation for many, many Toscano dishes.*

PISELLI con PORRI

PEAS with LEEKS

8 servings

2 pounds fresh peas

2 leeks, washed thoroughly, sliced

2 flowers of *nepitella* – catmint (or flowers of thyme)

1/4 teaspoon fennel seeds

1 cup chicken broth

1/2 teaspoon pepper

1/2 cup olive oil

Spritz red wine vinegar

Simmer shelled peas in enough water to cover them for 10 minutes. Add remaining ingredients and simmer another 10 minutes.

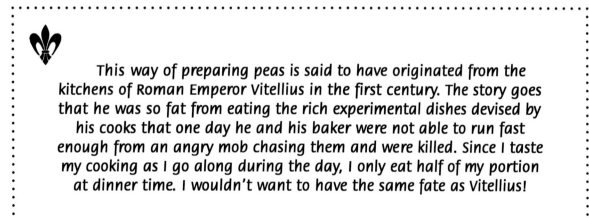

This way of preparing peas is said to have originated from the kitchens of Roman Emperor Vitellius in the first century. The story goes that he was so fat from eating the rich experimental dishes devised by his cooks that one day he and his baker were not able to run fast enough from an angry mob chasing them and were killed. Since I taste my cooking as I go along during the day, I only eat half of my portion at dinner time. I wouldn't want to have the same fate as Vitellius!

LATTE IMPERIALE

IMPERIAL CUSTARD

8 servings

1/2 cup *pignoli* – pine nuts

Spritz of brandy

> Roast pine nuts in shallow baking pan for 3 minutes in 500-degree oven. Remove pan and spritz a little brandy over nuts, stirring with a spatula. Roast 2 more minutes, take out; stir again and chop when nuts are cool.

3 cups *latte* – milk (half milk and half cream is even better)

4 eggs

3 tablespoons honey

1/2 teaspoon vanilla

A little *noce moscato* – nutmeg

> Rinse out a saucepan with cold water; add *latte,* scalding carefully by slowly raising temperature – do not boil. Beat eggs with wire whip; stir in honey and vanilla. Slowly pour *latte* into eggs, stirring continually. With ladle, divide the mixture into 8 custard cups. Sprinkle a little *noce moscato* and pine nuts over each cup. Add 1-1/2 inches water to a shallow baking pan and place cups in pan, arranged so that they don't touch each other or sides of pan. Place baking pan on the middle rack of a pre-heated 300-degree oven. Bake 1 hour; raise oven temperature to 325-degrees; bake 20 more minutes. Insert knife in the center of one to see if knife blade comes out clean. If not, bake another 5 minutes. Cool custard cups on wire rack; put foil over the tops and refrigerate.

Mamma made similar custard that she called Latte Portoghese. She thought it came from Portugal, but Apicius described this dessert being made in Rome 2,000 years ago, long before the Roman Legions got as far as Portugal!

Fattorino di Fiori

Looking forward to a convivial evening of intellectual stimulation, poet Dante Alighieri trudged along a dusty road in the valley leading to *il Castello del Re* – the King's Castle. As he walked, he enjoyed observing the vineyards, delighted by the sight of grapevines wrapping their arms around supporting trees. The grapes were just beginning to ripen, and Dante smiled in anticipation of the good wine that he knew would be served at dinner. A *fattorino* – messenger – from Re Roberto – King Robert – had presented a parchment scroll inviting Dante to the banquet earlier in the day.

When he arrived at the massive wooden door of the castle, Dante stomped his dusty boots and loosened his frayed, dun-colored cloak. One of the servants escorted him into the candle-lit banquet hall. As Dante bowed to Re Roberto at the head of the table, the King whispered something in his servant's ear. To Dante's astonishment, he was led down the entire length of the hall to the end of the table. Extremely offended by this insulting seating assignment, the poet refused to sit and departed immediately.

Re Roberto's guests gasped at the sight of the famous personage leaving in a huff. When the king was made cognizant of his blunder, he dispatched several servants to catch up with disgruntled Dante and beg him to return to the gala affair. Unmoved by their urgent voices, Dante hushed them and spoke: "Tell the king that I will return to the castle in my own time and on my own terms."

At the stroke of midnight, heralded by a triumphant trumpet *fanfara,* Dante dramatically re-entered the hall, clad in a magnificently jeweled *tunica*. The King smiled and clapped his hands in delight when he beheld his guest's extravagant clothes, pleading, "Dante Alighieri, I beg you to sit on my right at the head of the table." Dante responded, "I thank you for this great honor, my lord."

A servant rushed up to him, offering roast lamb upon a platter. Dante took a great slab of meat in his hands and vigorously rubbed the meat over his tunic. Blinking in disbelief, the servant placed a goblet of glorious purple-red wine before Dante. "*Grazie per il vino* – Thank you for the wine," declared Dante as he poured the entire contents of the goblet over the greasy meat stains on his tunic. Aghast, Re Roberto stuttered, "W-why? W-why? W-why do you ruin your gorgeous garment?"

"My gorgeous garment should be allowed to enjoy your food and wine," declared the poet, "since my *tunica* is the reason that I now have the honor to sit on your right."

After thinking this over for a few moments, the King replied, "I see your point. A man's worth should not be judged by his physical appearance, but by his character and knowledge."

"Guarda il calor del sol
che si fa vino
giunto all 'umor che de la vite cola."

"Observe the heat of the sun
making wine
as it combines with the liquid of the vine."

Dante Alighieri

1265 –1321

Pre-Renaissance poet Dante Alighieri, born in Firenze in 1265, believed in the virtue of the vernacular – common Italian language versus classic Latin. Extolling love and romance in his poetry, he also was concerned about divisiveness among people and wars between cities and countries. He constantly sought ways to bring about harmony and unification. While his epic, *La Divina Commedia – Inferno, Purgatoria e Paradiso* – The Divine Comedy – Hell, Purgatory and Heaven, is one of the most renowned works in the history of literature, his relatively unknown and unfinished book, *Convivio* – Banquet – affirms the spirit of the folk tale about Dante's "glorious garment."

In the *Convivio*, written around 1305, Dante frequently employed the words *carne e pane* – meat and bread – as metaphors for poetry and commentary. He described wisdom as being the "bread of the angels," and he declared that compassion is the "mother of generosity." He further advised that those who possess knowledge should bestow their wealth (knowledge) upon the disadvantaged. Dante felt that by doing so, the natural thirst of the needy would be quenched by the knowledgeable. He theorized about setting a special table, "A banquet for all men, with bread to accompany the meat."

Ruggero says, "Since I was a boy, I held Dante to be a fine, smart, humble gentleman. For a long time I have believed that the soul of every man is the knowledge that he gives to others. One of my favorite paintings depicts Dante waiting for his sweetheart Beatrice by the Ponte a Santa Trinita over the Arno in Firenze. Dante is dressed simply in a *tunica scura* – dark tunic, *cappuccio rosso* – red cape, and *sandali marroni* – brown sandals. Here in Markleeville, we *paesani* – country folk – also dress simply, usually in jeans and casual shirts. Guests at Villa Gigli, with dusty boots and wind-blown hair, who might have been fishing, hiking or soaking in nearby Grover Hot Springs, are welcome to join us for our *Convivio*."

MEDIEVAL MENU

· · · · · · · · · · · · · · · ·

PANE CAMPAGNOLO
COUNTRY-STYLE BREAD

ZUPPA di ZUCCA
PUMPKIN SOUP

QUAGLIE alla SALVIA
QUAIL with SAGE

CANNELLONI con CREMA ROSA
FILLED PASTA with ROSÉ SAUCE

ASPARAGI all'OLIO
ASPARAGUS with OLIVE OIL

AGNELLO ARROSTO
ROAST LAMB

PESCHE con VINO e MENTA
PEACHES with WINE and MINT

PANE CAMPAGNOLO

COUNTRY-STYLE BREAD

24 servings

2 packages dry yeast

1 cup tepid water

1/8 cup *madre* – mother (sourdough starter)

> In a bowl, dissolve yeast in tepid water. Stir *madre* into yeast. Cover with a clean white cloth and allow to rest for 30 minutes.

7 cups unbleached flour

1/4 cup mixed grains (five-grain cereal)

> Mix flour and grains together and heap on wooden counter, forming a *vulcano* – volcano. Drop the *madre* mixture into the *vulcano*.

3 cups tepid water

3 tablespoons olive oil

> Add liquids to *vulcano,* and with fingers of both hands incorporate into flour. Mix well and knead 15 minutes. Put dough in large bowl and cover with clean white cloth. Allow dough to rise 1 hour. Turn out on counter and knead for 5 minutes. Cover with cloth again; let dough rise 30 minutes.* Knead dough 2 minutes and form dough into an oval loaf. Place loaf on oiled 14-inch *pizza* pan. Cover with cloth and allow dough to rise 1 hour.
>
> Just before baking, gently cut a grid pattern on the surface of the loaf with a sharp razor blade. Bake 12 minutes at 500 degrees; lower temperature to 250 degrees and bake for 40 minutes; test with thermometer and if temperature inside bread has reached 190-degrees, it's finished. Cool on a rack for a few hours before slicing and serving.

Replace original madre by taking out 1/8 cup of dough. Madre can be stored in refrigerator for 2 weeks or so, until needed.

⚜ **This recipe is basic for not only my country-style bread, but for my Fettunta, Pizza, Schiacciata and Focaccia.**

ZUPPA di ZUCCA

PUMPKIN SOUP

8 servings

1/2 cup white wine

1 small pumpkin – about 3 pounds

> Cut pumpkin into sections; remove skin and seeds. Purée wine and pumpkin in blender; set aside.

1/4 pound dry *porcini*

2 cups hot water

> Soak *porcini* in hot water for 15 minutes; squeeze out water and chop. Reserve soaking water, except for the last gritty bit. Add to soup later.

SOFFRITTO – SAUTÉ (page 48)

4 ounces unsalted butter

2 cubes chicken bouillon, crushed

1 can (28-ounces) pumpkin

1/2 pint heavy cream

Juice and finely chopped peel of 1/2 tangerine

1/3 cup Amaretto

Pinch of pepper

Pinch of *semi di finocchi* – fennel seeds

> Stir butter into *Soffritto*; add *porcini* and soaking liquid, garlic and bouillon. Stir in pumpkin purée and other ingredients. Simmer slowly for 1 hour. Serve with *Fettunta*.

FETTUNTA — OILED BREAD SLICES

Most of the Toscano country people make Pane Campagnolo once a week. In my trattoria, I make Fettunta by cutting the loaf into 3/8-inch-thick slices, oiling and salting the tops, laying the slices out on pizza pans and putting them in a 500-degree oven for 5 minutes.

QUAGLIE alla SALVIA

QUAIL with SAGE

8 servings

8 quail, cleaned and ready to cook

MARINATURA – MARINADE

Juice of 8 tangerines

16 ounces white wine

> Marinate quail in juice and wine for two hours.

2 tablespoons pepper

1 cup olive oil

1 cup white wine

> Take quail out of marinade and dry them with paper towels. Sprinkle pepper inside cavities. Sauté birds on all sides in hot olive oil in oven-proof pan. Remove birds; add white wine and de-glaze the pan by scraping and stirring the browned bits into simmering wine with a spatula; reserve de-glazed wine in separate container.

8 slices *pancetta* – Italian bacon

8 twigs fresh sage

> Roll a strip of *pancetta* around each quail and place back in the pan. Drizzle de-glazed wine and place sage twigs over quail. Cover pan with aluminum foil and braise quail in 300-degree oven for 1 hour.

ASPARAGI all'OLIO

ASPARAGUS with OLIVE OIL

8 servings

24 asparagus

> Steam in upright steamer or in basket steamer with very little water for 5 minutes.

Juice of 2 lemons

1/2 cup olive oil

1/4 cup *prezzemelo* – Italian parsley – chopped

> Drizzle lemon juice and olive oil and sprinkle parsley over each trio of asparagus.

CANNELLONI con CREMA ROSA

FILLED PASTA with ROSÉ SAUCE

8 servings

RIPIENO per CANNELLONI – FILLING for PASTA

1/4 cup olive oil

1/4 onion, chopped finely

2 eggs, beaten

1/2 cup small peas

1 cup string beans, chopped

1 cup broccoli, chopped

2 cloves garlic, chopped

4 tablespoons honey-roasted sunflower seeds

Finely chopped peel of 1/4 orange

Finely chopped peel of 1/4 lemon

1/2 cup chopped celery heart

1 cup white beans, cooked, mashed

2 ounces blue cheese, crumbled

1/4 cup Swiss cheese, grated

1/4 cup smoked Gouda cheese, grated

1/2 cup New York cheddar cheese, grated

3 cups or less, Jack cheese, grated

Sauté onion lightly and add to other ingredients in a large bowl; mix with one hand while drifting a snowfall of grated cheese down with the other hand, mixing for 10 minutes. (Recipe continued on next page.)

FRITTATA al FORNO – OVEN-BAKED OMELET

Even though this filling is too much for 8 cannelloni, it's the only way to achieve the conglomeration of all of these flavors. Whatever is left over can be mixed with 4 beaten eggs and mashed into a baking pan. Cover and refrigerate overnight. The next morning bake in 300-degree oven 30 minutes for a Frittata al Forno – Oven-Baked Omelet.

CREMA ROSA – ROSÉ SAUCE

1 pint heavy cream

2 teaspoons Amaretto

1 small can (5.5 ounces) tomato juice

1 teaspoon pepper

Handful roasted *pignoli* – pine nuts

> Stir cream, Amaretto, tomato juice and pepper together and pour 1/4 of the *crema* into a baking pan.

CANNELLONI – FILLED *PASTA*

Tagliatelle dough (page 41), cut 4-inches-wide by 14-inches-long

> Have a big pot of boiling water ready, with one-tablespoon olive oil added. One at time, drop *pasta* pieces into boiling water. When they return to the surface, remove with slotted spoon to a clean, white towel. When all of the *pasta* pieces have cooked and cooled a bit, form *Cannelloni*. Take a handful of *Ripieno;* form it into the shape and size of a jumbo egg; place it on the *pasta* strip and roll *pasta* around *Ripieno*. Place the 8 *Cannelloni* over *Crema Rosa*. Pour remaining *Crema* evenly over *Cannelloni;* cover with foil; bake 25 minutes at 450 degrees. Before serving, sprinkle a few roasted pine nuts and distribute sauce left in pan and pine nuts over each *Cannelloni*.

AGNELLO ARROSTO

ROAST LAMB
8 servings

6-pound de-boned leg of lamb

MARINATURA – MARINADE
8 cloves garlic, chopped coarsely

1 bottle white wine

1/2 cup olive oil

Sprinkling of pepper

> Marinate lamb overnight in the refrigerator.

ARROSTO – ROAST
2 carrots, cut in thirds

12 sage leaves

12 garlic cloves

> Place lamb in large roasting pan; reserve marinade. Roast in 500-degree oven for 10 minutes; turn over and roast another 10 minutes. Remove from oven; make 12 small cuts on the top. Insert one clove of garlic and one sage leaf into each cut. Add marinade and carrots to the pan. Cover; roast at 350 degrees for 1 hour. Cool for 15 minutes. Slice in 3/8-inch slices.

When the famous 13th century artist Giotto was a young boy watching his family's sheep near Vicchio, he passed the time by sketching lambs on rocks with charcoal. Members of the Medici family strolled by and were amazed to see the boy's artistic ability. With his father's permission, they took Giotto to Firenze to study art. And that's how a simple country boy grew up to become a leader in Renaissance art and architect of the beautiful Campanile di Giotto in Firenze.

PESCHE con VINO e MENTA

PEACHES with WINE and MINT

8 servings

1 bottle Zinfandel, 3 years old or older

8 teaspoons honey

4 peaches, peeled, pitted and sliced

24 leaves mint, rinsed

8 flowering lavender stems (optional)

Pour 4 ounces of Zinfandel in each of the 8 wine glasses; add 1 teaspoon honey to each; stir together. Add peaches and top each glass with 3 leaves of mint and 1 lavender stem. Let the flavors conglomerate for one hour and then serve as the *finale* – finish – for your own *Convivio*.

A long time ago, around 1298, a young man named Castruccio Castracani decided to leave his home in Lucca to seek his fortune. He intended to join the military because he loved riding horses and brandishing swords. In his haste to embark on his adventure, the youth neglected to pocket any food or money. After trudging along a dusty road through the Chianti hills on his way to enlist, he came to the Val di Greve and entered the small town of Nozzole.

Tired, hungry and very thirsty, Castruccio Castracani sat down under a shady tree to rest. Since he had no money to buy bread or wine, he tied a string to a jar and lowered it into the depths of a well to get a little water to drink. Though his stomach was growling from hunger, he managed to sleep through the siesta hours. When *paesano* – peasant – Piero Pierini walked over to his well and saw the young man drinking water from the jar, he said, "You look like a fine young man, but I don't think that water is appropriate for you to drink. You should have a glass of my good red wine."

Castruccio Castracani responded sadly, "Alas, I have no way to pay for wine, so I am content to drink your pure water." Piero Pierini insisted, "Please accept my *vino rosso* – red wine – and also a couple of pieces of *focaccia* – flat bread – as my gift before continuing your journey."

Gratefully accepting his kind offer, Castruccio Castracani quenched his thirst with *vino* and quelled his hunger with *focaccia*. He told his benefactor, "I would like to give you my lance as a token of payment for the food that you have given me." Piero Pierini answered, "I appreciate your gesture, but since you're on your way to join the army, you must keep your lance. Without your weapon, misfortune might follow you forever." Castruccio Castracani was so touched by the peasant's sincere goodwill that he wrote down the man's name and town in his notebook: "Piero Pierini, Nozzole, Val di Greve."

Years later, after fighting in the constant clashes between the opposing factions of Guelfi and Ghibellini, the much wiser and wealthier Castruccio Castracani was elected Governor of Lucca. Following a big battle in Altopascio, when the Lucchesi had defeated the Fiorentini, hundreds of prisoners were lined up for the governor to review. As Castruccio Castracani passed along the rows of the enemy, he commanded each prisoner to state his name and place of birth. One weather-beaten old man looked straight into his eyes and clearly stated, "My name is Piero Pierini. I am from the town of Nozzole, in the Val di Greve."

Castruccio Castracani stopped in his tracks and embraced the old man. "Piero Pierini, I have never forgotten your kindness when you gave me *vino* and *focaccia*. I hereby grant you your freedom. Are there any other prisoners here from the Val di Greve?" Piero Pierini counted off on his fingers: Leoni Leoniero, Astancollo Astancolli, Paolo Panchetti, Renzo Rocci and Lelio Landi.

Castruccio Castracani asked those men to step up to the front of the formation. "You five are also free to go. May God be with you all."

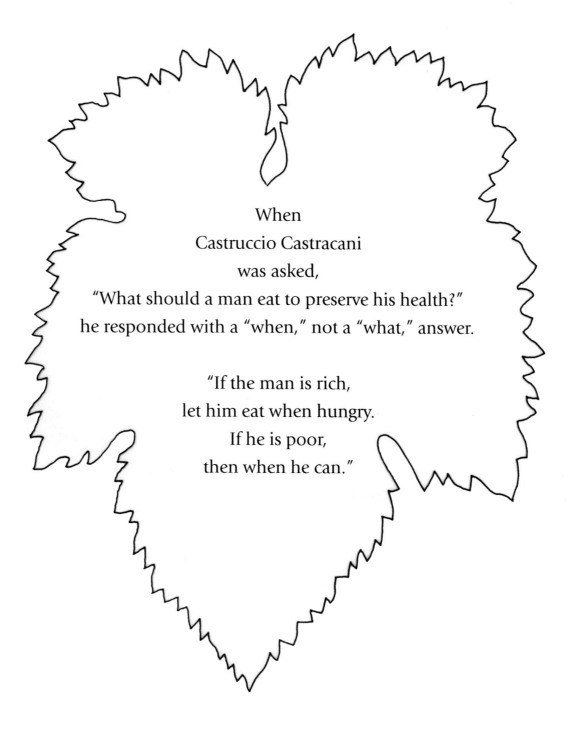

When
Castruccio Castracani
was asked,
"What should a man eat to preserve his health?"
he responded with a "when," not a "what," answer.

"If the man is rich,
let him eat when hungry.
If he is poor,
then when he can."

Castruccio Castracani has been described as a man who knew how to achieve power and use it. He was the thinly-disguised central character Niccolo Machiavelli featured in his 1505 masterpiece *The Prince*, still a basic text for Western political science.

After leading the Lucchesi in their defeat of the Fiorentini in 1325, Castruccio Castracani made certain that all of the wounded from both sides were given medical treatment. The battle had been disastrous, with many casualties, but the monks in the ancient monastery of Altopascio had always welcomed the sick, wounded, weary, lost or hungry.

Two years after the war, in 1327, when most of the patients had either recovered from their wounds or died, the monks installed a huge bell in the *campanile* – bell tower. Every evening at twilight, one of the monks would climb into the tower and pull the rope. The sound of the bell alerted anyone in the area that the brothers within the monastery were willing to share sanctuary and food with those outside the walls. This hospice is thought to have been the model for all of the others established throughout Europe, providing medical care for invalids and shelter for travelers or the homeless.

Each day the monks of Altopascio went into their garden to harvest ripe vegetables. If there weren't enough vegetables for dinner, the monks ventured out into the countryside with big sacks on their shoulders and asked neighboring farmers to donate produce. The monks chopped the vegetables and threw them into a huge *calderone* – kettle. They cooked the concoction very slowly to allow the natural flavors to blend together harmoniously. Visitors to the monastery were invited to sit down alongside the monks at long, wooden tables, break bread, sip wine and enjoy eating the delicious vegetable soup brewed in the *calderone*.

The citizens of Altopascio still gather together once a year to assemble a huge *calderone* in honor of Castruccio Castracani and the day when he conquered the Fiorentini in 1325. The *festa* has been named "*Calderone*" in honor of the monks' caldron of vegetable soup.

MONASTERY MENU
· · · · · · · · · · · · · · · · · ·

FOCACCIA al RAMERINO
ROSEMARY FLAT BREAD

CALDERONE MESCOLONE
VEGETABLE SOUP

PASTASCIUTTA IN BIANCO
NOODLES with WHITE SAUCE

CENCI
SWEET FRIED NOODLES

FOCACCIA al RAMERINO

ROSEMARY FLAT BREAD

2 rounds

1/2 portion *Pane Campagnolo* dough (page 58)

1/4 cup olive oil – or more, if needed

3 twigs rosemary, 2 chopped finely and the other left whole

Generous sprinkling of salt

Take 1/2 of the dough from *Pane Campagnolo* recipe and turn out onto counter. Form 2 round balls and cover with clean, white towels and allow to rest for 5 minutes. Flatten with rolling pin into flat, circular shapes, 1/2-inch-thick. Place each round on oiled 14-inch-diameter *pizza* pan. Cover with towels and leave for 10 minutes. Preheat oven to 500 degrees. With fingertips, push indentations into dough and put into oven immediately. After 5 minutes, take them out; turn them over and bake another 5 minutes. Remove from oven and turn them over so that the indentations are on top. Using a twig of rosemary for a brush, generously spread olive oil over tops and sprinkle with salt and chopped rosemary. Put them back in the oven for 5 minutes.

Focaccia is good to have on hand when friends drop by. It can be half-baked ahead of time, 5 minutes on each side; cooled; wrapped in plastic and stored in the freezer. When friends arrive, simply pre-heat your oven to 500 degrees; take focaccia from the freezer; thaw for 15 minutes; add olive oil, salt and rosemary and bake 5 minutes.

The name *focaccia* derives from the word *fuoco* – fire.
Old-time bakers would place a piece of flat dough
in the middle of the oven to test the *fuoco*.
If the dough burned,
the floor of the oven was swabbed with a wet mop
to cool the temperature.
If the dough took too long to bake,
more wood was added
to raise the temperature.
Today, the names *focaccia* and *schiacciata* are
interchangeable.

CALDERONE MESCOLONE

VEGETABLE SOUP

16 servings

BUON BATTUTO – GOOD CHOPPED VEGETABLES (page 48)

3 additional celery stalks, sliced

4 additional carrots, sliced

4 small zucchini, sliced

1 bunch Swiss chard, chopped

1 bunch spinach, chopped

3 cups cooked *cannellini* – white beans (See recipe for *Cuori di Palme,* page 31)

2 medium-sized potatoes, cut in strips 1-inch-long, 1/4-inch wide and 1/4-inch thick

8 cups water

1 cup red wine

Black pepper

> Add to *Buon Battuto* and simmer slowly for 2 hours, stirring now and then. Simmer 15 minutes and ladle into rustic soup bowls.

⚜ With a large bowl of this **zuppa**, a slice or two of **Pane Campagnolo**, and a glass or two of **vino rosso**, you can have a simple, satisfying supper.

PASTASCIUTTA IN BIANCO

"DRY" NOODLES with WHITE SAUCE

8 servings

PASTASCIUTTA – "DRY" NOODLES

Tagliatelle recipe for 8 (page 41)

Set aside 1/4 amount of this dough to make a dessert of *Cenci* (page 76).

8 cups water

*Drop fresh Tagliatelle (or store-bought "fresh" fettucini) into boiling water; when the water re-boils, drain the pasta and put into large, warmed bowl.

IN BIANCO – WHITE SAUCE

8 ounces unsalted butter

1 cup heavy cream

Small dash of nutmeg

1 cup grated dry Jack cheese

1 teaspoon white pepper

Slowly melt butter in top of *bagnomaria* – double boiler; add cream and *noce moscata* – nutmeg; stir together until thickened. Pour over *pasta* and stir sauce in. Divide onto 8 warmed plates; sprinkle cheese and pepper over each portion.

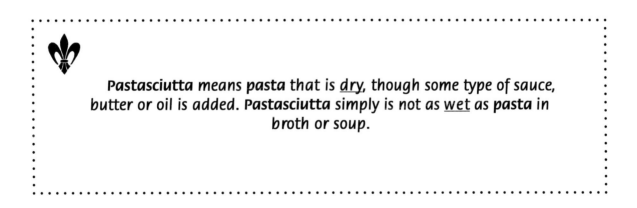

Pastasciutta means pasta that is <u>dry</u>, though some type of sauce, butter or oil is added. Pastasciutta simply is not as <u>wet</u> as pasta in broth or soup.

CENCI

RAGS

(SWEET FRIED NOODLES)

8 servings

1/4 recipe for *Tagliatelle* dough (page 41)

Roll out and s-t-r-e-t-c-h the dough thinner than usual. Cut into irregular pieces about 2-inches by 3-inches, to look like scraps from the rag-bag.

1 cup, or more, olive oil (1/2-inch deep in the frying pan)

1/2 cup sugar

One at a time, throw 4 "rags" (pieces of *pasta*) into hot oil. When the fourth "rag" has been added, turn over the first and keep up that sequence. When the first one is cooked crisp and light almond-colored on both sides, remove it to a platter. Cover with two layers of paper towels; add another one to the oil; keep on turning and adding until they are all cooked. Sprinkle sugar over both sides and serve while warm. Actually, they are almost as good when cold.

LAMINATION

Over the years I have developed a special secret method of rolling out my pasta, unknown except to a few friends and now to readers of this book. I laminate the pasta by adjusting the rollers for increasingly thin dough, folding the dough in half and turning it 90 degrees each time before I send it through the rollers, achieving "firm yet tender" pasta.

A delicate grapevine named *Malvasia* – white wine variety – lovingly twined her arms around old *Olivo* – olive tree – and whispered to him, "I love you more than I love life."

Grape leaves in the terraced vineyard began fluttering in the breeze as the different types of vines gossiped. Big red *Nebbiolo* – red wine variety – murmured to stout *Sangiovese* – red wine variety – "*Malvasia* is so foolish to cling to that old *Olivo*."

Sweet *Moscato* – white wine variety – nodded in agreement. "We must warn *Malvasia* about the perils of that unhealthy relationship."

Malvasia overheard the rustling of the leaves, but she continued to embrace *Olivo* as she wafted a message over the wind to the rest of the vineyard. "We are content in our relationship and request that you grant us privacy."

"But we only want to give you the benefit of our experience," whispered *Moscato*, "If you would consider allowing the *vignaiolo* – grape grower – to replace frail and feeble *Olivo* with a sturdy stake to support you, we would stop pestering you."

Sangiovese added, "Here we are all proudly marching straight and tall down the rows, securely held by our grape stakes, and you're flailing around, hanging on by your very tendrils to that gnarled old tree."

"I will not listen to any of you," shrieked *Malvasia*, as she clung to her lover. "I adore my beloved *Olivo* and I will remain with him forever!"

Suddenly, a whoosh of wind whirled around the hill headed in the direction of the vineyard. The ancient arms of old *Olivo* creaked and cracked. He groaned and moaned in agony. He lost his footing and was uprooted. As *Malvasia* twined her tendrils tenaciously around her aged lover, *Olivo* crashed down to earth, smashing *Malvasia* to her untimely death.

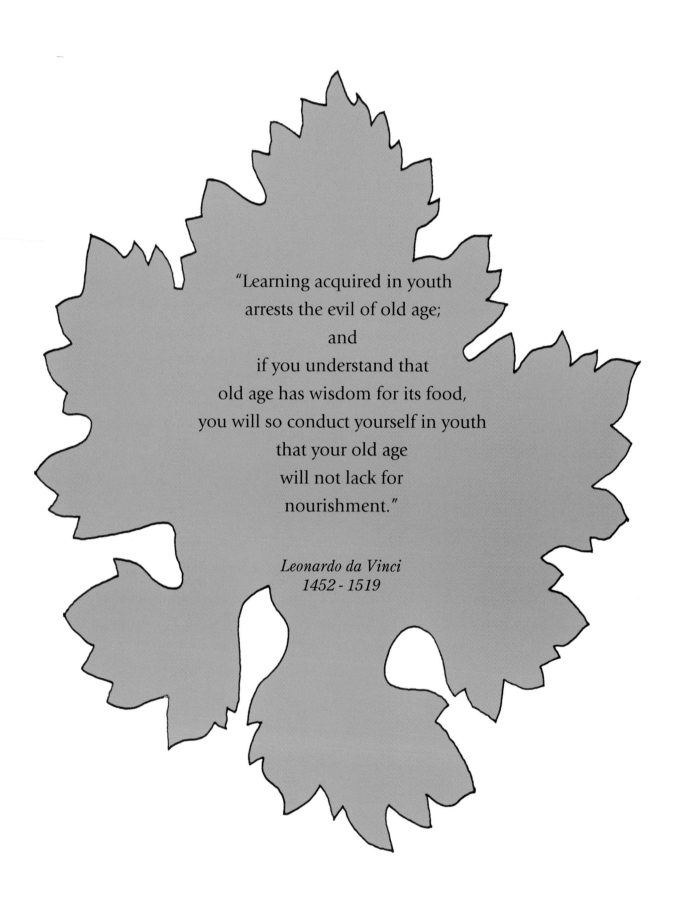

"Learning acquired in youth
arrests the evil of old age;
and
if you understand that
old age has wisdom for its food,
you will so conduct yourself in youth
that your old age
will not lack for
nourishment."

Leonardo da Vinci
1452 - 1519

Renowned "Renaissance Man" Leonardo da Vinci was the first person to record the fable about a grapevine and her supporting tree, though he used different words and names and no doubt wrote it in his distinctive mirror-image writing. *Arbustum,* the method of training grapevines up trees, has existed from the days of the Roman Empire until the present. In recent years, however, grapevines are more often trained on wooden or cement posts.

When we made our first pilgrimage to Leonardo's birthplace of Vinci, a small town in the hills above Firenze, the place was deserted. Since his stone house was closed, we wandered around the perimeter of the property and I sketched his front door. As we looked around, we speculated that the unusual atmospheric perspective of the hills and the oddly shaped cypress trees must have been major influences for Leonardo's paintings. Surrounding the house were ancient and gnarled olive trees, appearing as if they had been planted during the Renaissance. However, none of these trees were supporting grapevines!

Five years later, when we visited Vinci again, the wooden door to the house was open. We were awed to be allowed to enter Leonardo's tiny and unpretentious childhood home. One of my favorite quotations by Leonardo da Vinci is, "Small rooms or dwellings discipline the mind. Large ones weaken it." Since we live in a very small house on a hillside, designed by my architect father Frank W. Green, we couldn't agree more with Leonardo's philosophy.

After a few moments of silent contemplation spent in calling forth images of the Artist's early life, we drove along a narrow, winding road to the tiny village of Bacchereto. We couldn't believe our eyes when we encountered a larger stone house, with a small sign stating, "*Casa natale de la nonna di Leonardo da Vinci* – Birthplace of the grandmother of Leonardo da Vinci." According to the plaque, his grandmother's name was Lucia di Ser Piero di Zoso. Now the place is an inn, restaurant and wine cellar collectively known as Cantina di Toia. The restaurant was closed at that time of day, but we sat outside with a large stone wheel from an olive oil mill serving as our table. The host generously brought forth a bottle of red wine and fig cookies for a *spuntino* – snack. We returned ten days later for a memorable family dinner in the *cantina.*

RENAISSANCE MENU

· · · · · · · · · · · · · · · · · · · ·

PROSCIUTTO alle NOCI

HAM with WALNUTS

ZUCCHINI in UMIDO

SIMMERED ZUCCHINI

TORTELLINI ala FUNGHARELLA

TINY TWISTS of FILLED PASTA with
MUSHROOM SAUCE

STRACOTTO

"OVERDONE" ROAST BEEF

FRAGOLE del BOSCO

WILD STRAWBERRIES

PROSCIUTTO alle NOCI

HAM with WALNUTS

8 servings

1/4 pound *prosciutto* – Italian ham – sliced paper-thin

16 walnuts, shelled, separated in fourths

> Cut *prosciutto* into strips, approximately 2-inches by 6-inches. Wrap each strip around a walnut piece. Arrange in circular pattern on a plate garnished with rosemary blossoms, sage leaves, or other edible flowers.

ZUCCHINI in UMIDO

SIMMERED ZUCCHINI

8 servings

4 medium-sized *zucchini*, sliced 1/4-inch thick

1/4 cup olive oil

> Slowly sauté *zucchini* in olive oil for 10 minutes.

4 cloves garlic, sliced

> Throw in garlic and sauté for 2 minutes.

1 can (5-1/2 ounces) tomato paste

5-1/2 ounces warm water

> With wire whip, blend water and tomato paste and add to pan.

1/2 teaspoon salt

1/2 teaspoon pepper

1/2 teaspoon fennel seeds

> Stir in seasonings, simmer for 20 minutes and serve hot.

TORTELLINI ala FUNGHARELLA

TINY TWISTS of FILLED PASTA with

MUSHROOM SAUCE

8 servings

PASTA – DOUGH

Recipe for *Tagliatelle* (page 41)

Cut into 4-inch by 4-inch squares.

RIPIENO – FILLING

1/2 cup olive oil

1/2 pound fresh *porcini* mushrooms, chopped coarsely

1/2 pound ground beef

1/2 pound ground pork

2 teaspoons Bourbon

Chopped peel of 1/2 lemon

8 garlic cloves, chopped

2 cups dry Jack cheese, grated

> Sauté mushrooms 5 minutes. Throw in beef and pork; slowly sauté 10 minutes. Add other ingredients, except cheese; simmer 10 minutes. Cool for 1 hour. Stir cheese into cooked ingredients. Put 1 tablespoon *Ripieno*, into the center of each square. Pull edges together; form into *Tortellini* shape – be creative – as long as edges are sealed completely. Have a BIG pot of boiling water ready; throw the *Tortellini* in. As *Tortellini* come up to the surface, remove them with a slotted spoon into a large *pasta* bowl.

SALSA – SAUCE

> Very, very gently pour *Salsa Fungharella* (page 85) over the *Tortellini*; mix gently; portion onto 8 plates. Sprinkle a little grated dry Jack cheese (1/2 cup total) and a little pepper over each serving.

SALSA FUNGHARELLA

DRIED MUSHROOM SAUCE
8 servings

SOFFRITTO per la SALSA – SAUTÉ for SAUCE

8 ounces olive oil

8 ounces unsalted butter

8 cloves garlic, minced

Pinch of fresh sage, minced

> Sauté slowly for 5 minutes.

12 baby artichokes, chopped

24 black olives, minced

> Add to garlic mixture and continue to sauté slowly another 5 minutes.

1/2 pound dried *porcini*, soaked in hot water, drained, chopped

Juice of 1 lemon

> Add to other ingredients and sauté 10 minutes.

1 tablespoon Dijon-style mustard

Splash of Bourbon

1 teaspoon honey

Pinch of salt

Pinch of pepper

Pinch of fennel seeds

> Stir ingredients together with a wire whip; add to sauce; cover and simmer 20 minutes. Pour over *Tortellini*.

⚜ *Seated at a rustic wooden table, with rough linen napkins and hand-thrown terra cotta dishes, our dinner in the Cantina di Toia was so perfect that we will never forget the evening. Arrigo, the son of the owners, had a studio down the hill where he had made all of the pottery for the trattoria. To recreate a similar Renaissance setting, use earthenware dishes – try using glazed terra cotta flower pot saucers (checking that the glazing is lead-free and safe for food service), unbleached muslin napkins tied with ribbons and flower petals scattered over a country pine table or redwood picnic table.*

STRACOTTO

"OVERDONE" ROAST BEEF

8 servings

4-pound sirloin tip roast

MARINATURA – MARINADE

2 cups *Sangiovese* – red wine

1/2 cup olive oil

> Marinate roast 24 hours; covered, in refrigerator. Remove and *rosolare* – sear – 5 minutes each side in skillet. Place meat in 12″ x 10″ x 5″ pan.

SOFFRITTO – SAUTÉ (page 48)
BUON BATTUTO – GOOD CHOPPED MIXTURE (page 48)

> Add *Buon Battuto* to *Soffritto* and slowly sauté 10 minutes.

2 bouillon cubes, dissolved in 1 cup hot water

1 cup *Sangiovese*

> Add to *Buon Battuto*; pour over meat. Roast, covered, 300 degrees, for 2 hours. Pour *Buon Battuto* in bowl to cool. Mix in blender to make a *sugo*, or sauce. Slice meat in 1/2-inch-thick portions. Warm *sugo* in small pan, if necessary, and pour over each serving of *Stracotto*.

FRAGOLE del BOSCO

WILD STRAWBERRIES

8 servings

40 small strawberries, if not wild, tender and ripe

1 small bottle *Moscato* – Muscat wine (white)

1 lemon, cut into 8 wedges or slices

> Remove tops from strawberries, and marinate them in the *Moscato* for 1 hour or more. In small dishes, arrange 5 strawberries with their juice and wine and add a lemon slice on the edge of each dish.

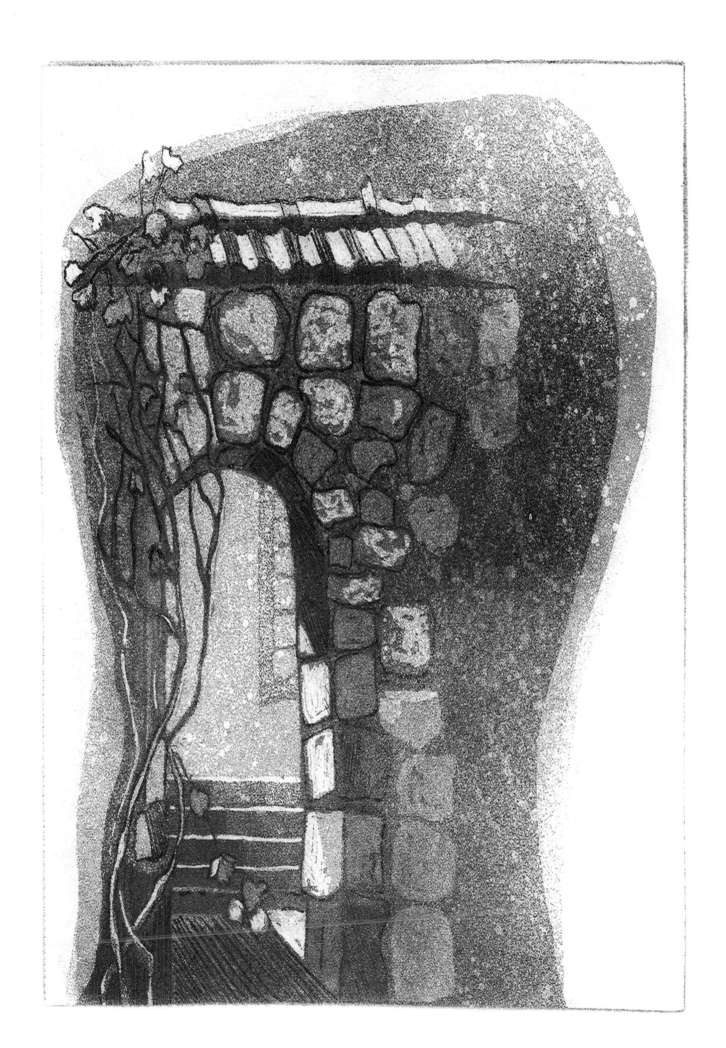

Giovanni Giovannini sighed as he thought about the long day ahead of him. He was the *torrigiano* – lighthouse keeper – for the city of Livorno in Tuscany. Renaissance times of the early 1500s were intellectually stimulating for philosophers, poets, writers, sculptors, painters, scientists, students and teachers, but not for Giovanni Giovannini.

Giovanni grumbled to his friend Cipriano Cipriani, "Here I am, stuck in this tower by the sea, at the *Bocca d'Arno* – Mouth of the Arno River – with nothing to do all day except to fish. With these silly government rules, I'm not even allowed to use olive oil from my lantern to fry the fish I catch."

Cipriano Cipriani raised one eyebrow and inquired, "What are you complaining about? You receive an adequate salary and you have the best view in town!"

"I'll tell you why I'm complaining. The *sindaco*, our mayor, is not only stingy with *soldi* – money – but also with *olio di olivo* – my personal allotment of olive oil. Am I allowed to fry fish with this oil? No! This beautiful green-gold olive oil must be used <u>only</u> to keep the lamps lit all night for the ships at sea!"

"Of course you must keep the lanterns glowing. Would you have ships run aground? These are special times for international shipping and Livorno is a very important port."

"Yes, yes, I know all of that," replied Giovanni Giovannini, "but do you think that the authorities really would care if I used *poc'olio* – a little oil? Though I'm not allowed to use great amounts of oil to fry my fish, perhaps I could think of a better way to prepare each day's fish catch."

"That's the spirit!" encouraged Cipriano Cipriani. "Tonight I'll reward your improved attitude by bringing you a gift of fresh *aglio* – garlic – and *nepitella* – catmint – from my garden."

Giovanni Giovannini thanked him and added, "That reminds me, yesterday some sailors from a large ship arrived in port and they gave me two types of strange produce from America. One fruit is round and yellow, called *pomo d'oro* – golden apple (tomato). The other vegetable, *peperoncino* – chili pepper – is fiery hot. I think I'll sauté your herbs in a teeny bit of olive oil, throw in the sailors' strange stuff and add my *caccia* – fish catch. I'll boil it all in sea water for a salty and savory soup."

Giovanni's soup is called *Cacciucco* – pronounced <u>ca-chu-co</u>. Tradition calls for at least five types of fish; one fish for each of the five seas and for each "C" in the name <u>CACCIUCCO</u>.

In the New World

"They made bread out of little fishes
which they took from the sea,
first boiling them, (then) pounding them,
and making thereof a paste, or bread,
and they baked them on the embers;
thus did they eat them.
We tried it,
and found that it was good.
They had so many other kinds of eatables,
and especially of fruits and roots."

Amerigo Vespucci
1454-1512

Famous Renaissance explorer, Amerigo Vespucci, was born in 1454 in Tuscany, in the tiny medieval hilltop town of Montefioralle overlooking the larger town of Greve. As we know, the continent of America was named for this adventuresome navigator.

Relatively unknown is that two other names for America were also considered: *Colombia* in honor of Cristofero Colombo, born in Genova in 1451, and *Verrazzana* in recognition of Giovanni da Verrazzano, born in Greve in 1485.

Amerigo Vespucci sailed along the north shore of South America in 1499, discovering the Amazon River, among other landmarks. He was as unsuccessful in finding a hoped-for western passage to Asia as Verrazzano and his Genovese friend Colombo had been. The last Vespucci descendant was buried in the 19th century in Montefiorelle. Since most of the inhabitants have left for easier living in the valley, the population in the fortified old town is now less than 100.

Verrazzano was the only one of the three famous navigators who actually explored the eastern coast of North America. He sailed there in 1524, landing at a place now known as Cape Fear in North Carolina. Since he was the first adventurer from the Old World to discover the Hudson River, the Verrazzano Bridge in New York is named for him.

Purely by coincidence, Giovanni da Verrazzano came from the neighboring town of Greve, center of the Chianti Classico viticultural area. It's amazing to think that two inland, small-town dwellers left their peaceful olive groves, wheat fields and vineyards to venture out upon turbulent seas in search of wild and unexplored lands.

Castello da Verrazzano in Greve, birthplace of Giovanni, was built in the early 15th century, but his family line also died out in the 19th century. The castle now belongs to Luigi Cappellini, a Florentine restaurateur and producer of Chianti Classico wines. Olive groves and vineyards surround the venerable castle, while an immense rusted anchor rests in the courtyard entrance serving as a monument to commemorate Giovanni da Verrazzano, the restless Renaissance explorer who actually landed in North America.

MARINA MENU
· · · · · · · · · · · · · · ·

CROSTINI al PESTO
BASIL TOASTS

SCAMPI al MANDARINO sopra TAGLIERINI
TANGERINE SHRIMP over NARROW NOODLES

CACCIUCCO
FISH SOUP

SPUMONI con MOSTARDA
FRUITED FROZEN CREAM with BERRY SAUCE

CROSTINI al PESTO

BASIL TOASTS
8 servings

PESTO – CRUSHED BASIL SAUCE

2 cups basil, finely chopped by hand

8 cloves garlic, chopped

1/2 cup pine nuts, chopped

1 cup olive oil

Juice and finely chopped peel of 1 lemon

1 teaspoon salt

1 cup finely grated Jack cheese

Rinse and dry basil with cotton cloth. Stir first six ingredients together with a wooden spoon. Warm over hot water in *bagnomaria* – double boiler. Stir in cheese at the last moment.

CROSTINI – TOASTS

8 slices *Pane Campagnolo* (page 58), cut into small squares

Lightly toast bread squares on both sides and spread *Pesto* over.

One wintry night in Porto Fino in a tiny, quiet **trattoria** by the marina, I learned to make pesto. My own addition to the recipe is lemon juice and grated peel. I do this to add a little bitter flavor and also to preserve the green color of the basil. Pesto over pasta is wonderful also! I use a simple storage system, called <u>sott'olio</u> – under oil – when I need to preserve good fresh basil. Chop up basil; pour equal amount of good olive oil over; stir together; pour into ice cube trays. When cubes are frozen, place tray in plastic bag and keep in freezer until needed.

SCAMPI al MANDARINO sopra TAGLIERINI

TANGERINE SHRIMP over NARROW NOODLES
8 SERVINGS

SOFFRITTO per SCAMPI – SAUTÉ for SHRIMP

1 cup olive oil

4 garlic cloves

16 sage leaves

> Pour oil into large, shallow baking pan and add garlic and sage leaves. Heat in 400-degree oven for 10 minutes.

SCAMPI – SHRIMP

16 large *scampi* – shrimp – cleaned, de-veined

Juice of 1 *mandarino* – tangerine

1/2 cup red wine vinegar

> Add *scampi* to hot oil in the baking pan, turning them over to coat with oil. Drizzle *mandarino* juice and vinegar over *scampi* and braise them in the oven for 15 minutes, 400 degrees.

TAGLIERINI – NARROW NOODLES

Dough from *Tagliatelle* recipe (page 41)

> Cut rolled-thin-dough into strips 1/8-inch-wide by 8-inches-long. Throw into boiling water. When the water re-boils and the *Taglierini* come up to the surface, drain and gently mix with the *scampi*. Divide among 8 plates and serve hot.

CACCIUCCO

FISH SOUP

12 servings

50 mussels

50 clams

25 large shrimp, de-veined and pre-cooked

2 pounds *calamari* – squid (tentacles only)

1 crab, cleaned and pre-cooked

1 pound red snapper, skin and bones removed

4 teaspoons salt

> Bring 1 gallon of water to boil in large pot; drop in mussels, clams, shrimp, squid, crab and snapper. Simmer 15 minutes.

SOFFRITTO – SAUTÉ (page 48)

> Add to the pot.

24 garlic cloves

1 pound snow peas, chopped

3 leeks, sliced lengthwise, 1-1/2 inches long

1/4 pound dry *porcini*, soaked, drained, chopped

Juice and grated peel of 1 lemon

1 can (28 ounces) crushed tomatoes

1/2 cup *Sangiovese* – red wine

Pinch red pepper flakes

> Add ingredients to the pot; simmer 4 hours. If desired, place a slice of *Fettunta* (page 59) in the bottom of each bowl; pour *Cacciucco* over bread.

SPUMONI con MOSTARDA

FRUITED FROZEN CREAM with BERRY SAUCE
12 servings

1 pint heavy whipping cream

1/4 cup honey

1/4 cup brandy

10 drops lemon extract

10 drops orange extract

1 cup mixed dried fruit – raisins, cranberries and figs

> Whip cream until almost stiff, 7 to 10 minutes. Stir in other ingredients. Spoon into small custard cups; cover each cup with aluminum foil and place in freezer for one day. The next day, uncover and pour a thin layer of *Mostarda* over each (page 97). Cover again and return them to the freezer until ready to serve, at least 2 hours later. If keeping frozen for any length of time, store in tightly sealed plastic.

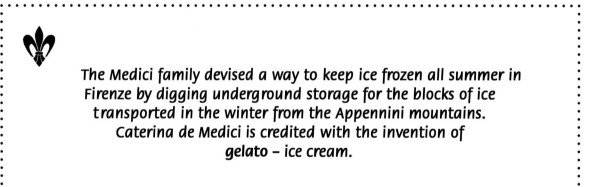

The Medici family devised a way to keep ice frozen all summer in
Firenze by digging underground storage for the blocks of ice
transported in the winter from the Appennini mountains.
Caterina de Medici is credited with the invention of
gelato – ice cream.

MOSTARDA

BERRY SAUCE

"many servings"

1/2 pound ripe black grapes

1/4 pound ripe blackberries

1/8 pound ripe strawberries

3 cups old Zinfandel

Chopped peel, pulp and juice of 1 orange

> Coarsely chop grapes and berries with a little of the wine in a bowl. Peel orange; chop peeling and pulp; reserve juice. Place fruit in large pan and add orange juice and the remaining Zinfandel. Bring to a simmer and cover with lid ajar, cooking slowly for 2 hours.

4 fresh bay leaves, chopped

1 cup honey

Pinch of nutmeg

> Add honey and bay leaves; simmer another 2 hours. Add pinch of nutmeg near the end of the cooking. Cool and store in refrigerator in covered container for up to 2 months.

The main reason that I make Mostarda is to create a layer of frozen sorbetto over hand-made Spumoni. Pour a little Mostarda over the already-frozen Spumoni, previously portioned into custard cups, and re-freeze after tightly covering each cup with plastic wrap or foil.

Mostarda, named for the mosto – must or juice of the grapes – can be poured over other desserts and also over roasted meats. The sweetness of the grapes, combined with the tartness of the blackberries, contributes to the complexity of Mostarda.

Ruggero remembers
going into the *castagneto* –
chestnut woods – with his Mamma to
gather *porcini*.
He always trusted her intuition about which
mushrooms were good and which were not.
For a test, she would sauté
a sample of the mushrooms
along with some garlic in hot olive oil.
If the garlic turned coppery-green,
she considered the mushrooms poisonous
and she would throw them all away.
Now he doesn't trust anyone's intuition,
but safely buys
dried darkly smoked
boletus mushrooms
from the
Mendocino Mushroom Company.

Though wealthy banker Niccolo Castelvetro had provided his son Giacomo Castelvetro with handsome clothes, fine food and one of the best libraries in 16th century Modena, Italia, the seventeen-year-old boy was in trouble again.

Religious reformation was just one of the subjects that young Giacomo read about and discussed with his tutors. But he made the mistake of announcing his admiration of the Protestant cause in public, ruffling the feathers of a flock of Roman Catholic aristocrats.

One night as Giacomo was studying his books, he was disturbed by a cacophony of cackling in the courtyard. Looking up from his manuscript, he was startled when his father rushed into the room shouting, "Quickly, my son; there is no time to be lost. You must wrap this tapestry around your shoulders and follow me!"

Niccolo called to his servant, "Corrado Carotti, please bring a sturdy chest down to the library, one long enough to hold Giacomo."

"*Babbo* — Dad," howled Giacomo, "What's happening?"

Niccolo replied, "If you don't leave Italia at once, my son, you will be imprisoned for your heretical beliefs."

And so, in the dark of night, trusty Corrado Carotti led a caravan of mules bearing seven chests packed with seven tapestries plus one very frightened boy through the Alps to Geneva, Switzerland. Giacomo Castelvetro spent many years there, living with his uncle Lodovico, who also had been exiled by the Roman Inquisition. Castelvetro continued to travel throughout Europe for the rest of his life, studying and expressing his thoughts about many subjects in many languages, not only by teaching and tutoring members of royal families but also by writing scholarly manuscripts.

Near the end of his life, living alone in London, remembering his beloved Italy and witnessing what he considered to be the appalling diet of the English, Castelvetro wrote a manuscript entitled, *Breve Racconto di Tutte le Radici, di Tutte l'Herbe et di Tutti I Frutti, Che Crudi o Cotti in Italia si Mangiano* – A Brief Account of the Vegetables, Herbs and Fruit, Raw or Cooked That We Eat in Italy. He may have succeeded in his attempt to tempt the English to appreciate vegetables, because the English were truly enamored of Italianate culture during the 17th century. Four centuries later, many of us seeking a healthier diet are following Castelvetro's advice by eating less meat and more vegetables.

Insalata ben salata,
poco aceto e ben oliata –

Salt the salad quite a lot,
then generous oil put in the pot,
and vinegar, but just a jot.

Giacomo Castelvetro
1546-1616

Agricultural diversity typifies the Toscano countryside, as evidenced by the sight of stone walls framing terraces of olive trees interlaced with blocks of vineyards, fields of wheat and rows of vegetables. *Casa colonica* – farm house – and *castello* – castle – alike feature oil-stained grinding stones, ancient wine casks and wood-burning ovens as homage to the legendary "Mediterranean Trio."

Many California wine growers are entering into similar agricultural diversity programs by planting olive trees and encouraging cover crops such as mustard and *fava* – beans – to grow between vine rows. These cover crops are also good for soil-building when the vegetation is plowed back into the earth, making rich humus. It's a little-known fact that in the mid-19th century, when winter wheat and other grains were planted extensively in Napa County, more than one-tenth of all the grain in the United States was grown there.

Now, in Napa's Pope Valley, Juliana Vineyard's viticulturist Tucker Catlin is growing other crops to supplement his grape-growing. He is experimenting with designing low fences and hedgerows of blackberries to protect the vineyard and garden from foraging deer. He explains, "The deer don't want to get tangled up in the wires and berry bushes. Pest management is integral with this system because the berry habitat attracts the *Anagrus epos* wasps who in turn parasitize the leafhopper larvae. Our plant materials are chosen for their contributions, and we have bushes that attract pollinating butterflies. The vegetation is on our side!"

Celebrating the joys and benefits attributed to the Mediterranean Trio, Catlin hosted an Italian-style picnic by the lake in the vineyard for family and friends a few years ago. Ruggero cooked for this event, and I decorated the pavilion with hand-painted silk banners and streamers. The tables were laden with big bowls heaped with fruit and vegetables, field greens and edible flowers, *pasta* salad and *pizzas*. While a guitarist strummed and sang melodic Italian arias, children swam in the lake and their parents tossed *bocce* balls. I truly thought I was back in the hills of Chianti.

When I returned to my studio, I etched a fanciful landscape with images of grapes, grains, olives and other fruits and vegetables paradoxically layered in primitive/atmospheric perspective.

GARDEN MENU
· · · · · · · · · · · · · ·

PIZZA MARGHERITA

QUEEN MARGARET'S PIZZA

INSALATA di POMODORI

TOMATO SALAD

PASTA FREDDA con SALMONE AFFUMICATO

COLD NOODLES with COLD SMOKED SALMON

VERDURE in CARTOCCIO

VEGETABLES in PARCHMENT

TUTTI FRUTTI

ALL FRUIT

PIZZA MARGHERITA

QUEEN MARGARET'S PIZZA

8 servings

PANE – BREAD DOUGH

1/2 recipe *Pane Campagnolo* (page 58)

4 tablespoons olive oil

> Let dough rise for 45 minutes. Form into 2 balls, about 1-pound each; rise another 45 minutes. With hands, flatten each ball into a circle. With rolling pin, roll up and down circles twice. Turn circles 90-degrees; roll up and down again, until 3/8-inch-thick. Place dough-rounds on well-oiled 14-inch *pizza* pans, clear to the edges of pans. With fingertips, push indentations into dough, spaced about 2-inches apart.

COPERTA – TOPPING

1 can (28 ounces) crushed tomatoes, or 6 fresh tomatoes, thinly sliced.

2 cups fresh basil, torn in pieces

> Spread tomatoes over each crust, to the edges! Tear basil; sprinkle over.

2 teaspoons salt

2 teaspoons pepper

3 cups *mozzarella* cheese, grated

> Drift salt, pepper and cheese over tomato and basil topping, making sure to cover everything with cheese. Bake 550-degrees 8 to 10 minutes. Cool *pizzas* 5 minutes; cut each one into 4 wedges. Serve hot.

> *Simple pizza is the best! For pizzazz-pizza, I add a few crushed hot pepper flakes. Pizza goes back to Egyptian, Greek, Etruscan and Roman days when flat dough tested oven temperature. Salt, oil and seasonings were added later. The combination of tomatoes, basil and cheese is attributed to the Napoletani, specifically to Principessa Margherita di Savoia who married King Umberto I in 1899.*

INSALATA di POMODORI

TOMATO SALAD

8 servings

POMODORI – TOMATOES

4 red, ripe tomatoes, sliced

1/2 cup olive oil

2 teaspoons red wine vinegar

16 basil leaves, torn

1/4 onion, chopped finely

2 teaspoons pepper

1/2 teaspoon salt

> Cut tomatoes in 1/2-inch-thick slices; discard the "ends." Remove seeds and pulp. Arrange slices on platter. Sprinkle onion over. Spritz oil and vinegar over. Add salt and pepper. Turn each slice of tomato over and add another spritz of oil and vinegar and basil pieces. Cover plate lightly with plastic wrap and leave at room temperature for 1 hour before serving.

INSALATA – GREENS

1 pound mixed greens

> Rinse and dry greens very well and put into large mixing bowl. Sprinkle salt and pepper over; toss using wooden spoons; drizzle olive oil over, toss again; drizzle vinegar over, toss the third time.

TWO CHOICES

1.   Serve tomatoes and greens on separate dishes.

2.   Heap greens on serving platter. Arrange tomatoes around the edge.

PASTA FREDDA con SALMONE AFFUMICATO

COLD NOODLES with SMOKED SALMON

8 servings

Tagliatelle recipe (page 41) – or purchased "fresh" *fettucini*

> Throw *Tagliatelle* into big pot of boiling water. When water re-boils, drain *pasta*; rinse in cool running water; drain well. Cut *pasta* in 1-inch lengths.

1/2 onion, chopped

1/4 pound green beans, cooked *al dente*, chopped

1 stalk celery, chopped

1 red bell pepper, chopped

1 cup black-eyed peas, cooked

1/4 cup Mediterranean-style black olives, pitted and chopped

1/4 cup dried *porcini* – soaked, drained, chopped

4 garlic cloves, chopped finely

16 basil leaves, chopped

1 pinch dried red pepper flakes

Chopped peel of 1 lemon

1 teaspoon capers

2 tablespoons olive oil

1 teaspoon Dijon-style mustard

1 teaspoon pepper

1/2 cup dry Jack cheese, grated coarsely

1/2 pound smoked salmon

> Mix all ingredients together, stir in cold *Tagliatelle*; heap on 8 plates.

1/2 pound smoked salmon

> Top each serving with 3 additional chunks of salmon.

VERDURE in CARTOCCIO

VEGETABLES in PARCHMENT

8 servings

8 medium red ripe tomatoes, each cut in 4 slices

8 small potatoes, peeled and cut in quarters

8 small carrots, peeled and cut lengthwise, 2-inches by 1/4-inch

16 garlic cloves

1 pound fresh string beans, cut in 3-inch lengths

1 green, 1 yellow, 1 red bell pepper, cut in strips 1/2-inch wide

1 large onion, cut in slices 1/4-inch wide and 3-inches long

4 small crook-neck squash, cut in 2-inch by 1/2-inch strips

8 teaspoons chopped fresh *prezzemelo* – Italian parsley

Pinch of red pepper flakes

8 squares aluminum foil, 18-inches, and 8 squares parchment, 15-inches

1/4 cup olive oil

> Place parchment over foil. Brush olive oil in center of parchment (6-inch-circle). Place vegetables, in order given, in center of parchment.

1 cup olive oil

Juice of 2 lemons

2 teaspoons pepper

> Sprinkle olive oil, lemon juice and pepper over each portion. Pull corners of parchment up, forming a bundle and twisting corners together. Pull up foil the same way. Arrange packets on baking pan and cook on barbecue grill for 20 minutes or bake in 500-degree oven for 20 minutes. Discard foil before serving and arrange *Verdure in Cartoccio* on each plate.

TUTTI FRUTTI

ALL FRUIT

8 servings

1 peach

1 pear

1 apple

8 black figs

> Cut fruit into 1-inch pieces and put into a mixing bowl.

1 cup blackberries

1 cup blueberries

1 cup strawberries

16 mint leaves, torn in half

> Add the berries and mint to the fruit.

1 cup Port

3 cups old Zinfandel

2 cups sugar

> Stir gently into fruit. Cover bowl with plastic wrap. Refrigerate 24 hours before serving *Tutti Frutti* in stemmed wine glasses.

When Ruggero uses lemons and oranges
in his cooking,
he remembers Giacomo Castelvetro,
who wrote four hundred years ago
about using the juice and peel
of "bitter oranges" in cooking.

Lemons, oranges and tangerines
really add magic to other ingredients.

The mystery of the naming of Vin Santo Toscano is shrouded by the darkness of the Middle Ages. The Fiorentini – Florentines – and Senesi – Sienese – have different stories about the naming of their famous dessert wine, Vin Santo.

Fiorentini, who love to relate tales of intrigue whether the event took place yesterday or 650 years ago, say that the wine formerly known as *vin pretto* – pure wine – was tagged with the name Vin Santo in 1349.

During an Ecumenical Council attempting to unify the two schisms of the Catholic Church, a banquet was given in honor of Cardinal Bessarione, the Patriarch of the Greek Orthodox Church. When he tasted the amber-hued wine, he turned to Emperor John VII Palaeologus and pontificated, "*Ma questo e un vino santo!* – But this is saintly wine!"

The Senesi, quite naturally, have a different story.

During the Plague of 1348, when the citizens were traumatized by waves of illness and death inundating the city, families of the sick swarmed to the churches to pray for relief. A monk, wishing to be of some help to the dying masses, left his hilltop monastery and trudged down to the city to donate a special honey-sweet wine to the church. The priests thanked the monk for his wine donation and used it on Sunday for *la comunione*. On Monday, many of the afflicted began to recover, and soon the plague declined. "This monk's wine must be curing the hordes of sick people," claimed the citizens. In succeeding years, it therefore has become traditional to drink a little Vin Santo – saintly wine – for health's sake, at the end of dinner.

The Fiorentini and the Senesi, are in accord that Vin Santo is an excellent *digestivo* to enjoy after dinner. They only disagree as to the choice of vintners, because every Italian I've ever met thinks that his or her treasured bottle of Vin Santo is the very best!

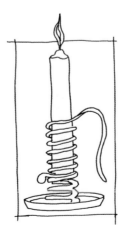

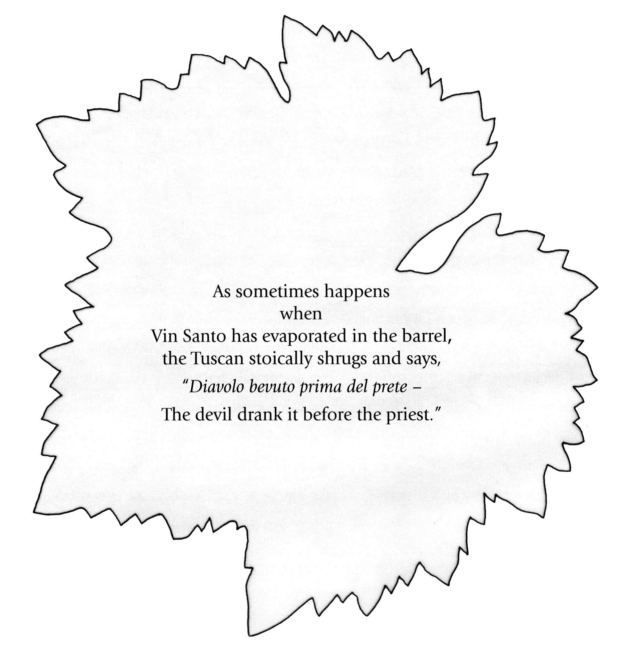

As sometimes happens
when
Vin Santo has evaporated in the barrel,
the Tuscan stoically shrugs and says,

"Diavolo bevuto prima del prete –
The devil drank it before the priest."

Today, all of the wineries producing precious Vin Santo follow parallel methods, with slight variations. The wine, sanctified-in-name-only, ferments and matures in exalted solitude in airy attics rather than keeping other wines company in crowded cellars.

The general practice is to harvest very mature grapes; dry the clusters on mats in well-aired rooms; press the grapes and pour the juice into *caratelli* – small oak barrels. Then the bung-holes are sealed with cement, and the barrels are left undisturbed in the attic for an incredible four to eight years, with no peeking allowed!

As I find the beauty in the Chianti district of Tuscany to be extraordinary, sketching wine cellars and vineyards is one of my most favored pastimes. On our last trip to Italy to visit Ruggero's family, our vinous explorations concentrated on the mystique of Vin Santo.

Enjoying the ensuing treasure hunt, we became especially fascinated by the history of the Marchesi de' Frescobaldi family. Even before the memorable East-West Church Conference, the Marchesi de' Frescobaldi were known as wine producers. Their noble family name has also been woven into the texture of Florentine history, with members having served as politicians, bankers, soldiers, explorers, poets and musicians.

In the middle of the 19th century, the properties of the Frescobaldi were united through marriage with those of the Degli Albizi family. Marchese Vittorio Degli Albizi used his viticultural knowledge to improve the family vineyards and also modified the Tuscan flask so that it could be hermetically sealed, thereby making it possible to export Chianti wine.

Marchese Leonardo Frescobaldi, in his brown suit and polished old leather shoes indicative of his modest and unassuming demeanor, met us at Castello Nipozzano and gave us an extensive tour of that hillside estate. Then he took us to the even higher-on-the-hill vineyards of his Pomino properties. The Frescobaldi had commissioned me to create three etching editions for them; one of the *sangiovese* grapevine, another of the *pinot bianco* grapevine and one of the *vinsanteria* – wine attic – all on their Pomino estate.

The immense attic, lined with row upon row of *caratelli*, was crowned with a *mattone e legno* – brick and beam – ceiling. Open windows framed views of terraced vineyards bordered by cultivated forests, olive groves and fields of grain. Upon returning home to Markleeville, we turned my pencil sketch of the attic into a limited edition *intaglio*. I etched the plates in nitric acid and Ruggero hand-pulled the prints on our large press.

The Marchese told us that the Frescobaldi style of making Vin Santo revolves around the practice of picking very mature grapes, as late into October as possible. The white grapes traditionally used are *trebbiano, malvasia, pinot bianco, pinot grigio* and in recent years, chardonnay. After the grape clusters have spent approximately 40 days spread out on cane mats, they are pressed, and the *mosto* is poured into the *caratelli* without completely filling the barrels. A little *madre* – mother – or long-aged wine that has decreased in quantity and increased in alcohol is added. The bungs are sealed airtight before Christmas.

The barrels, nested in their aerie, experience the cold of winter and the heat of summer. The interior liquid responds by alternately slumbering and awakening or being dormant and then fermenting. When we were there in the summer, I put my ear next to a barrel and heard the soft sound of fermentation.

After four years or more, when fermentation stops and the alcohol is 15 to 18 percent, the barrel is broached in hope that an ambrosial wine will be drawn out. The yeasts that feed on the *mosto* will have expired from over-nourishment. If no sugar is left, the wine is dry, but if there is residual sugar, the wine is sweet. Dry Vin Santo may be served as an *aperitivo*, but if it achieves the hoped-for sweetness, it becomes a perfect *digestivo*, accompanied by *Biscotti da Vino* – cookies to dip in the wine.

With Vin Santo, there is always the excitement of uncertainty. The winemaker might encounter a wine to treasure or a vinegar to trash. Or, upon broaching the barrel after so long a time, a layer of sediment might indicate evaporated liquid, the only evidence of what might have been.

SUMMERTIME MENU
· · · · · · · · · · · · · · · · · · ·

SALSA di POMAROLA sopra TAGLIATELLE
TOMATO SAUCE over NOODLES

POLLO al MATTONE
CHICKEN under BRICK

BISCOTTI da VINO
COOKIES for WINE

SALSA di POMAROLA

TOMATO SAUCE

8 servings

1/4 cup olive oil

2 ounces butter, sliced

1/4 onion, chopped

3 cloves garlic, chopped

<u>Summer</u>: 8 medium-sized fresh red tomatoes, chopped

<u>Winter</u>: 1 can (28-ounce) crushed tomatoes (without seasoning)

Juice and chopped peel of 1/2 lemon

1 tablespoon pepper

> Lightly sauté onion in the olive oil and butter; stir in garlic and add the remaining ingredients; simmer for 15 minutes; shut off heat.

1/2 bundle basil, chopped

> Stir in basil and pour hot sauce over hot *Tagliatelle* (page 41).

In the summer, I use only fresh tomatoes from the garden; if not from my garden, from someone else's garden. In the winter, I use canned, crushed tomatoes because store-bought winter tomatoes aren't too tasty. Recent studies say that tomatoes, especially those that are processed, are loaded with a compound called lycopene. This substance provides a good defense against certain cancers and also reduces the risk of heart attacks. So we just continue to enjoy healthy **Pomarola** sauce throughout the year, whether the tomatoes are from the garden or the can.

POLLO al MATTONE

CHICKEN under BRICK

8 servings

4 Cornish game hens

> Cut chickens in half and then cut the wings off so that the *pollo* will lie flat under the bricks when grilled on the barbecue. Reserve wings to make *brodo al pollo* – chicken broth. Cut off all skin and fat.

MARINATURA – MARINADE

1 cup olive oil

1 sage twig, chopped

8 garlic cloves, chopped

> Marinate *pollo* in olive oil, sage and garlic for 2 hours.

GRIGLIA – GRILL

8 clean, washed bricks

8 sage twigs

> Throw sage into <u>hot</u>, glowing coals of grill. Sprinkle some salt and especially lots of pepper over each game hen and place on the grill. Put a brick over each game hen to flatten it, retain juices and ensure even cooking. Grill for 5 minutes and then turn over, replacing bricks on top, for another 5 minutes. Repeat steps twice more for a total of 20 minutes of grilling.

> *Though I realize that everyone has a favorite way to grill, I'll just say that I never buy manufactured charcoal briquettes, but prefer to burn branches of pine, mountain mahogany and bitter brush from the forest around here. When we lived in Napa Valley, I often used old wine-soaked barrel staves, along with split oak. Also, I use matches instead of starter fluids and let the wood burn down to charcoal.*

BISCOTTI da VINO

TWICE-BAKED COOKIES for WINE
120 COOKIES

1 tablespoon olive oil

6 cups flour (hold in 1 cup in reserve)

3 cups granulated sugar

2 teaspoons baking soda

Pinch of salt

> Preheat oven to 375 degrees. Oil four 14-inch *pizza* pans with olive oil; dust with flour. Mix dry ingredients together; heap on counter. Make a crater in the flour.

6 eggs + 2 extra yolks

1 teaspoon each of vanilla, almond, orange and lemon extracts

Coarsely grated peel and juice from 1 orange and 2 lemons

3-1/2 cups toasted, coarsely chopped almonds

1/2 cup pine nuts

12 ounces chopped dried figs, stems discarded

> Beat eggs with fork, add extracts, peel and juice; pour into crater. With hands, slowly conglomerate dry mixture into liquids working from the center outward. Sprinkle reserved flour over counter to prevent sticking of dough. Work dough until well blended.

> Slowly add nuts and figs. Knead 15 minutes. Divide dough into 4 balls. Divide each ball into thirds and roll long sticks, 2-inches in diameter, in lengths to fit *pizza* pans. Place 3 rolls on each pan.

> Bake 375 degrees, 30 minutes. Halfway through baking, reverse pans. Slide rolls onto counter with spatula. Cut diagonally in 1/2-inch slices. After baking both batches of *Biscotti*, reduce temperature to 300-degrees. Arrange *Biscotti* with cut sides up on the pans and bake an additional 10 minutes. *Biscotti* taste best when dipped in Vin Santo.

When Barone Bettino Ricasoli, owner of Castello di Brolio winery and vineyards near the village of Radda-in-Chianti graciously gave us a personal tour, we were appreciative. We had driven many miles from Firenze along the Via Chiantigiana to reach Brolio, relating stories to each other of the ancient rivalry and bloody battles between Siena and Florence. Because each town was so prideful of its domain, it puzzled us to lean over the crenellated parapet of the Barone's castle and see the rooftops of Siena. When we asked the Florentine Barone why the border between the ancient citadels was selected so close to the Siena city limit, a smile crept over his noble countenance, and he related the following fable.

Two opposing political powers, Guelfi and Ghibellini, clashed constantly. A bitter argument escalated from a dispute about the location of the border between Siena and Firenze. Representatives from each *senato* – senate – held a joint conference, but could not agree upon a fair method of delineating the boundary between the two provinces.

"The border should go along the ridge of the hill," declared Niccolo Niccolai.

Berardo Beradi shouted, "No, the line should follow the river's course!"

"The defined line should occur midway between the two cities," said Sergio Settesoldi.

"You're right," agreed Niccolo Niccolai, adding, "But how can the midpoint be found?"

"I have the perfect solution," declared Lando Landini. "Each city will select a trusted *fattorino* – messenger – and provide him with a swift horse. The border will be set at the place where the two riders meet. The horses will be saddled tonight to gallop the Via Chiantigiana tomorrow morning."

Niccolo Niccolai questioned, "But how will we know that they will leave at the very same time?"

Wise Lando Landini settled the matter once and for all. "Each rider will depart at dawn's first light when he hears the rooster crow." Guelfi and Ghibellini both agreed to the plan.

Unfortunately for the Senesi, the *furbo* – clever – Fiorentini instructed their *fattorino* to creep out quietly to the chicken coop a full two hours before the anticipated sunrise. The Florentine rooster, black as ink in the protective cloak of darkness, watched as the *fattorino* lit a lantern in the doorway. On cue, the rooster crowed and the Florentine *fattorino* jumped on his horse and sped down the Via Chiantigianna to meet his astonished opponent close to the walls of Siena. To this day, the *gallo nero* – black rooster – attests to Florentine resourcefulness by appearing on labels of Chianti Classico.

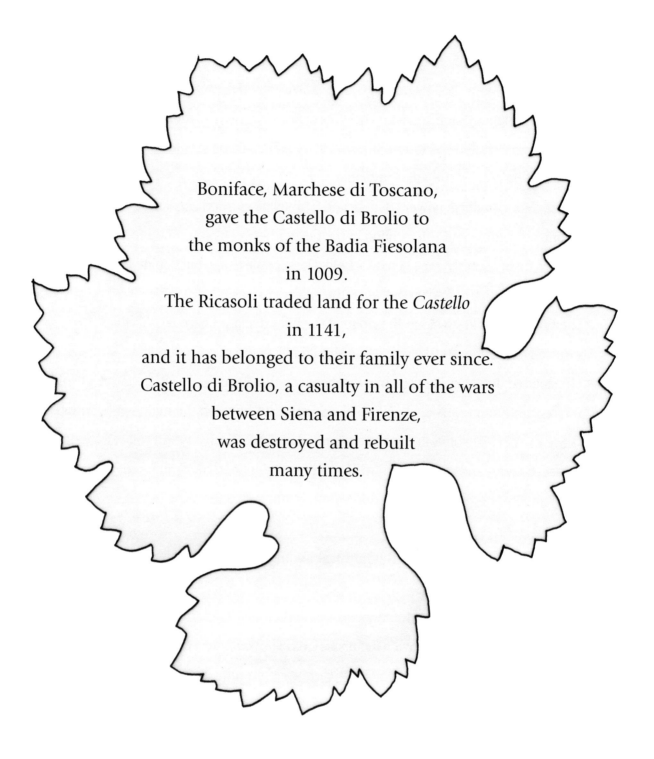

Boniface, Marchese di Toscano,
gave the Castello di Brolio to
the monks of the Badia Fiesolana
in 1009.
The Ricasoli traded land for the *Castello*
in 1141,
and it has belonged to their family ever since.
Castello di Brolio, a casualty in all of the wars
between Siena and Firenze,
was destroyed and rebuilt
many times.

Paleobotanists have ascertained from fossil evidence that ancestral wild vines grew in the region now recognized as Chianti some tens of thousands of years ago. Archaeologists have deduced that wine was produced in the Chianti area long ago in the Etruscan era from clay pot fragments.

The Chianti wine territory has been recognized since the 1200s and officially delimited in 1932. Siena province claims 414 square miles of Chianti Classico, and Firenze province claims 304 square miles.

Landscape artists are drawn to the area by the harmonious juxtaposition of valleys and forested hills. Woods are composed of oaks, chestnuts, domestic and maritime pines, cypress and several varieties of resinous conifers. Villages, vineyards, olive groves and cultivated fields of grains and grasses, enhance these pastoral scenes. Wild boar, hare, pheasant, deer and partridge abound in such a diverse habitat. The main grape varieties grown in the rolling vineyards are *sangiovese, canaiolo, trebbiano* and *malvasia.*

Genteel Barone Bettino Ricasoli, current head of the family and *padrone* – owner – of Castello di Brolio and Cantina di Brolio, pulled the rope at the one and only gate to the castle, and a man servant descended to let us in. The Barone took us into the historic family chapel, the only original section of the castle not destroyed by battles and fires. After admiring the colorful mosaics in the apse of the chapel, we peered down through a round grate to the tombs below.

Later, when we toured the winery, I couldn't resist asking the Barone about a legend I had heard of one of his ancestors, also named Barone Bettino Ricasoli, and his connection with Chianti wine. Ruggero kicked my ankle to deliver a "stop" message, but my question had already become a "go."

"Is it true that your great grandfather, nicknamed the 'Iron Baron,' imprisoned his bride here in this castle and then, to distract himself, developed and refined the formula for Chianti Classico?"

I had been told that the 'Iron Baron' married a very young and extremely beautiful Florentine noblewoman. As newlyweds, they attended a grand ball in Firenze, where she danced and flirted outrageously all evening with scores of handsome young men. The jealous "Iron Baron," his patience exhausted, firmly propelled his bride to the door. He draped her cape over her shoulders, escorted her to their carriage and shouted *"Andiamo a Brolio!"*

The carriage rolled down the Via Chiantigiana to Castello di Brolio, arriving at dawn. According to legend, the Barone imprisoned his young wife in the castle tower for life. Never again would she flirt with the Florentine dandies.

The current Barone Ricaloli dismissed the story with a sigh. *"Imposibile,"* he remarked. "The Via Chiantigiana was not in existence at that time, and carriages could not travel without roads. Since gentlemen rode on horses and ladies were transported by porters in chairs, the trip would have taken days, not hours. The truth is that my great-grandfather Bettino moved to Brolio in 1830 as a practical matter of business. He found it necessary to restore order at the estate, since my widowed great-great grandmother, living in Firenze, had neglected it. He and his wife did stay nine or ten years here, while he revolutionized vineyard and winery techniques. He encouraged crop rotation and used his marketing expertise for the advancement of Chianti wine."

Now that we know the true story, Ruggero and I just smile when we hear legends about the "Iron Baron" and his "sequestered" wife .

COUNTRYSIDE MENU
. . . .

CROSTINI di TRE COLORI

TOASTS of THREE COLORS

TAGLIERONI al POLPETTONE

WIDE NOODLES with MEATLOAF

SPINAGI all'AGLIO

SPINACH with GARLIC

NECCI con COPERTA di CREMA

CHESTNUT FLOUR PANCAKES with
COVER OF CREAM

CROSTINI di TRE COLORI
TOASTS of THREE COLORS
24 servings

SALSA VERDE – GREEN SAUCE

1/3 recipe for *Crostini al Pesto* (page 93)

> Spread over 24 squares, 2 x 2-inch toasted pieces of *Pane Campagnolo* (page 58), or 24 toasted slices of sourdough baguette.

SALSA ROSSA – RED SAUCE

1 red bell pepper, very finely chopped

4 ounces butter

1 tablespoon Dijon mustard

Pinch of pepper

Dash of Amaretto

> Slowly sauté chopped red pepper in butter 10 minutes; remove pan from heat; stir in other ingredients. Spread over 24 toasts.

SALSA NERA – BLACK SAUCE

1 can (3.8 ounces) sliced black olives, drained and finely chopped

1 can (2 ounces) fillets of anchovies, drained and chopped

6 cloves garlic, chopped

1/4 cup olive oil

> Mix all ingredients together; spread over 24 toasted toasts.

CROSTINI – TOASTS

> Arrange *Crostini* in alternating rings of green, red and black on a round platter, fringed by herbs and flowers.

POLPETTONE in TEGLIA

MEATLOAF in a PAN

8 servings

1/2 onion, chopped, lightly sautéed

1 pound extra lean ground beef

4 eggs

1 pound grated Jack cheese

Chopped peel of 1/4 lemon

4 garlic cloves, chopped

1 teaspoon pepper

1 teaspoon Worcestershire sauce

2 teaspoons pine nuts

2 teaspoons honey-roasted sunflower seeds

1 teaspoon chopped leaves of *nepitella* – catmint – or thyme

In large bowl, mix ingredients together. Use clean hands to mix everything well. Pat meat mixture evenly in 1-1/2″ layer in an oiled 13″ x 9″x 2″ disposable aluminum foil pan. Nest two pans together for extra strength. (Throw pans away after *Polpettone* is cooked; no tough cleaning job at end of dinner!) Cover with foil; bake 20 minutes, 500 degrees. Bake another 15 minutes uncovered after lowering the temperature to 300 degrees. Remove from oven and pat surface with crumpled paper towels to absorb excess oil. Put *Polpettone* back in oven, uncovered; bake another 15 minutes. Cut loaf in half lengthwise first, then cut crosswise 3 times to make 8 portions. Serve with *Taglieroni al Polpettone* (page 131).

SUGO di CARNE

MEAT SAUCE

8 servings

1/4 pound ground pork or sausage

1 pound ground beef

BUON BATTUTO – GOOD CHOPPED VEGETABLES (page 48)

Stir meat into *Buon Battuto*. Simmer 20 minutes.

1 can (12 ounces) tomato paste

3 cups warm water – reserve 1 cup to use if sauce becomes too thick

1 ripe tomato, chopped

6 garlic cloves, chopped

1 cup cooked black-eyed peas

1 broccoli top, chopped

3 medium-sized carrots, sliced horizontally

1/2 bundle fresh spinach, chopped coarsely

Juice and chopped peel of 1/2 lemon

Pinch of hot pepper flakes, and a dash of pepper

Sparse dusting of nutmeg

Small bay leaf, crumbled

1 ounce brandy

Stir tomato paste and water together with wire whip; stir into meat sauce.

Add remaining ingredients, and simmer slowly uncovered for 3 hours.

TAGLIERONI al POLPETTONE

WIDE NOODLES with MEATLOAF

8 servings

Tagliatelle recipe for 8 (page 41)

Cut freshly made dough into strips 1-inch-wide and 12-inches-long. Place individual portions of half-cooked *Taglieroni* in 8 small disposable aluminum pans.

Polpettone recipe for 8 (page 129)

Add a small chunk of *Polpettone* over each portion of *Tagliatelle*.

Sugo di Carne recipe for 8 (page 130)

Pour 2 ladles of *Sugo di Carne* over each portion. Cover with foil and bake at 450 degrees for 30 minutes.

> When I cook **Sugo di Carne** in the morning, I ladle some of it over slices of **Pane Campagnolo** for lunch. This **sugo** goes over any kind of **pasta**.

SPINAGI all'AGLIO

SPINACH with GARLIC

8 servings

2 bundles fresh spinach

Rinse leaves carefully; throw in boiling water and stir for a couple of minutes. Drain; squeeze water out by pressing down with a wooden spoon on spinach in strainer. Heap spinach on cutting board and slice horizontally and then vertically.

1/2 cup olive oil

8 garlic cloves, chopped

Light sprinkle of salt

Sauté garlic very lightly; add spinach and sauté 5 minutes.

NECCI con COPERTA di CREMA

CHESTNUT FLOUR PANCAKES with COVER OF CREAM

8 servings

3 eggs

2 tablespoons water

Grated peel of 1 lemon

Mix eggs, water and lemon peel with wire whip.

1/2 cup chestnut flour

2 cups unbleached flour

1 cup water

2 tablespoons olive oil

Sift in chestnut flour, unbleached flour; add water. Continue mixing with wire whip until smooth. When olive oil is hot in frying pan, pour 1 full tablespoon of batter at a time, leaving 1 inch between each thin pancake. After pouring the 4th pancake, turn over the first one. They should be light-almond-colored on both sides. Serve on warmed plates. Drizzle honey over for breakfast. For dessert, layer with *Coperta di Crema* – Cover of Cream (page 133).

My first job was cooking chestnuts when I was eight. I wanted to go to the movies, but I didn't have any money. I got the courage to ask, "Mamma, could you give me one lira?" She answered my question with a question. "How will you pay me back? If I give you one lira now, when you return home I want to see two lire!" After the movie, I knew that I couldn't go back home unless I brought Mamma two lire. I asked Signora Giovanna, who was roasting *marroni* – chestnuts – on the street, if I could help her for two lire. I have always remembered the lesson that I learned from Mamma – whenever you borrow, always pay back MORE."

COPERTA di CREMA

COVER of CREAM

8 servings

1 pint *ricotta*

1/4 pint heavy cream

2 teaspoons Amaretto

Spoon *ricotta* into bowl, add cream and Amaretto and mix with wire whip for about three minutes.

This mixture can be used to layer with *Necci* – small thin chestnut flour pancakes – or as a topping for pastry desserts.

4 teaspoons chocolate syrup

When making two layers of *Necci* and *Coperta di Crema*, drizzle a little chocolate syrup over the *ricotta*.

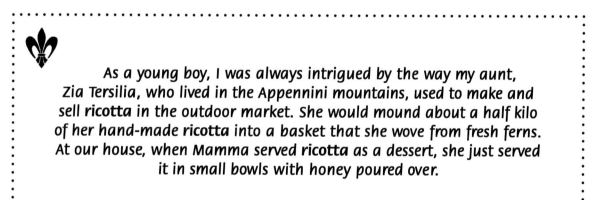

As a young boy, I was always intrigued by the way my aunt, Zia Tersilia, who lived in the Appennini mountains, used to make and sell ricotta in the outdoor market. She would mound about a half kilo of her hand-made ricotta into a basket that she wove from fresh ferns. At our house, when Mamma served ricotta as a dessert, she just served it in small bowls with honey poured over.

RICETTE FONDAMENTALI
BASIC RECIPES

<u>Unbleached flour</u>
for
various shapes and sizes
of
Pane (page 58) and *Pasta* (page 41)
and
<u>Fresh produce</u>
for
Soffritto (page 48) and *Buon Battuto* (page 48)

"Napoleone and his soldiers are approaching Borgo San Lorenzo!" shouted Bruno Bruni from the doorway of the *macelleria* – meat market – having just been told this incredible news by the *funaio* – ropemaker – Pinucchio Panchetti. Across the street, the *ciabattino* – cobbler – Siro Squiloni warned, "We have to keep the French soldiers from occupying our town, but they're heavily armed." Chino Chini, the *carrettaio* – carriage maker – yelled down the *vicolo* – lane, "What can we do to protect ourselves?"

From her window above the *macelleria*, Tina Tucci was pegging newly washed clothes on a line stretching above the street to the balcony over the *ciabatteria* – shoe repair shop. When she heard all of the shouting, she called down to the growing knot of men, "If you men heap stones to throw at the French, we women will do our part to defend our town." Tina Tucci shouted a message to Dorina Dori who called to Fernanda Ferrini who shrieked at Bianca Bandini who yelled at Rolanda Romangnoli who cried out to Giselda Giraldi. "Get out all of your pots and pans and put the water on to boil!" The women of Borgo San Lorenzo sprang into action and stoked up the fires in their stoves, filled their pots and pans with water, and set as many to boil as they could fit on the burners.

When the French soldiers arrogantly marched through the town gates, leaders astride prancing horses, they were astounded to be met by volleys of sharp stones and torrents of scalding water. In panic, they fled, leaving the triumphant Borghese cheering.

Later in the afternoon, by way of celebration, the citizens gathered together in the *piazza*. The women carried down the same pots they had used to heat water and douse the invaders. While they waited for the water to boil over charcoal burners, they danced merrily around the *piazza*. As the water commenced to bubble and boil, they stirred *farina gialla* – cornmeal – into the pots for a communal feast of *polenta* — cornmeal mush.

Polenta, or cornmeal mush,
was unknown in the Old World
until Italian and Spanish explorers
brought maize back
from the New World
in the 16th century.

To this day, the citizens of Ruggero's hometown, Borgo San Lorenzo, celebrate Napoleon's retreat by hosting a free city-wide party called *"La Polentata delle Ceneri – The Polenta Party of Ash Wednesday"* – to mark the day in 1799 that the French Army fled north. Long tables, portable burners, and big copper pots of boiling water to cook the *polenta* are set up in Piazza Garibaldi.

When Ruggero was a young boy, he was occupied by a variety of jobs and had scant time to party. He sifted sand in the river and helped the *funaio* – ropemaker – by turning the wheel to twist hemp. He kept the fire going for the *maniscalco* – ferrier. When he was 12, he started working in the bakery of *Fornaino* – the little baker – as an unpaid apprentice from 3 a.m. to 7 a.m. and from 7 a.m. to 4 p.m. as a paid bread delivery boy, pedaling his three-wheeled bicycle.

Still, there were special days to enjoy. On *Lunedì di Pasqua* – Easter Monday – the townspeople traditionally trooped into the hills to picnic with leftovers from their big Easter Sunday dinner. After their picnic, they would enjoy their extra day of leisure by looking down at the beautiful panorama of the Valle del Mugello.

Ruggero says, "Harvest time was a very happy event because there was always an abundance of fruit and vegetables. In the fall, we also searched for *tartuffi* – truffles – under the *pioppi* – poplar trees. The people of Borgo San Lorenzo celebrated harvest with *La Festa della Raccolta* staged in the *piazza*. *Venditori* – vendors – cooked all kinds of food and sold produce, similar to farmers' markets that are popular in America now. The difference is that today buyers take home their vegetables to a refrigerator, while at *La Festa della Raccolta* people bought vegetables to store away for the approaching winter. If they didn't have a *cantina* for storage, they stashed potatoes, onions and garlic under their beds because their bedrooms were always the coldest rooms in the house. They needed those vegetables to last through the long winter."

FESTIVAL MENU

. . . .

INSALATA di CORIANDOLI

CONFETTI SALAD

POLENTA con PIGNOLI

CORNMEAL MUSH with PINE NUTS

CONIGLIO al DOLCE FORTE

RABBIT with SWEET and SOUR SAUCE

MELE al FORNO

BAKED APPLES

INSALATA di CORIANDOLI

CONFETTI SALAD

8 servings

2 heads butter lettuce

>   Wash; dry well; arrange 3 leaves on each of 8 salad plates.

2 heads fennel, inner white part only, diced

1/2 red pepper, diced

1/2 green pepper, diced

1/2 yellow pepper, diced

1 leek, sliced thinly, "circles" separated

8 cloves garlic, minced

Chopped peel of 1 orange

Juice of 1 lemon

1/4 cup olive oil

>   Mix everything together 30 minutes before serving.

16 walnuts, shelled, chopped

2 teaspoons salt

1 teaspoon pepper

>   Mound mixed ingredients in center of each plate. Sprinkle salt, pepper and nuts over.

POLENTA con PIGNOLI

CORNMEAL MUSH with PINE NUTS

8 servings

12 cups water

6 cubes chicken bouillon

4 garlic cloves, chopped

> Pour water into a big pot; turn heat high; stir in bouillon cubes and garlic.

3 cups coarsely ground *farina gialla* – coarsely-ground cornmeal

> When the water comes to a boil, turn the heat down to low. With one hand slowly pour in cornmeal, and with other hand and a long-handled spoon, slowly stir *polenta* continuously for 20 minutes, scraping sides and bottom of pan.

1/2 cup pine nuts

> Stir half of the nuts into *Polenta* and simmer another 5 minutes. Turn *Polenta* out onto oiled wooden chopping block. With a wet spatula gently form *Polenta* into a rectangular loaf approximately 2-1/2 inches thick. Spread second half of pine nuts over top of loaf and with wet spatula, softly press them in. After cooling 10 minutes, slice *Polenta* into 1/2-inch strips, using an oiled string. Place 2 slices on each plate.

> There are four Polenta variations you can use: Cover with *Sugo di Carne* or grated cheese and reheat; or drizzle with olive oil or honey and grill; or substitute for *Pane Campagnolo* in *Crostini* recipe; or serve with *Coniglio al Dolce Forte* - rabbit (page 143).

When Mamma made polenta, she gave me the job to stir while she heated the meat sauce and grated the cheese. I enjoyed this job very much for two reasons; because I liked the profumo – perfume – of the polenta cooking, and at the end, she let me clean the pan, so that I got an extra portion.

CONIGLIO al DOLCE FORTE
RABBIT with SWEET and SOUR SAUCE
8 servings

SALSA DOLCE FORTE – SWEET and SOUR SAUCE

1 cup olive oil

1 medium sized onion, chopped

8 garlic cloves, chopped

4 fresh sage leaves, chopped

1 bay leaf, crumbled

1 fresh sprig thyme, chopped

2 tablespoons fresh fennel leaves, chopped

1 teaspoon fennel seeds

> Sauté ingredients in olive oil over low heat for 30 minutes.

1 can (16 ounces) natural style fruit cocktail

1/2 pound muscat grapes, mashed

12 ounces bourbon

6 ounces red wine vinegar

Pinch of nutmeg

> Add these ingredients to the *Salsa*, and simmer for 2 hours.

CONIGLIO – RABBIT

1 rabbit about 2 pounds, legs and back, cut into 2-inch pieces

1 cup olive oil

> Sauté rabbit pieces in olive oil 7 minutes on each side in heavy ovenproof pan.

> Pour *Salsa Dolce Forte* over rabbit pieces; cover and roast, covered, at 400 degrees for 45 minutes. Serve over *Polenta*.

MELE al FORNO

BAKED APPLES
8 servings

8 Delicious apples

1/2 cup citrus honey

1/2 cup sugar

Pre-heat oven to 500 degrees. Cut about 3/4-inch off the bottom of each apple. Carve a cone-shape with a spoon down to the center of the apple, about 1-inch deep. After adding 1/4-inch of water in the bottom of a disposable aluminum baking pan, place apples in the pan, top-side down. Drizzle honey over apples, and it's okay, in fact it's good, if some spills down the sides.

8 boiled chestnuts, mashed

1/2 cup port

Mash chestnuts with port and divide among apples, spooning mixture over the honey. Sprinkle sugar over, like snow falling. Bake apples for 1 hour, 500 degrees. Remove from oven and cover with a reversed bowl for 1 hour to slowly steam apples.

Young Bacco – Bacchus – left home for an exploratory journey. One day after becoming very tired, he sat down under a tree to rest. When he woke from his nap, his eyes focused upon a solitary vine with beautiful leaves. He was intrigued by the intricate patterns and colors of the leaves and decided to transport the vine back home. Tenderly and carefully, he dug up the plant but worried that it would wilt.

"I'll put the vine into this thighbone from a bird," he said to himself, "to protect it from the sun's harsh heat." His botanical treasure flourished until shoots were springing out from each end of the bird bone.

"Oh, no. This will never do," he muttered, and stuffed the bird bone into a lion's thighbone. Soon leaves, shoots, tendrils and roots grew out of that bone, too.

Desperate to protect his precious vine, Bacco spotted the skull of an ass by the side of the road and inserted the lion bone, with the bird bone and vine, into the ass's skull.

When he returned home, the vine was entwined with the bird, lion and ass bones, so he dug a hole and placed roots and bones and all into the earth. To the delight of Bacco, the vine grew strong and tall. After three seasons, clusters of glorious grapes grew on the vine, and he crushed those grapes into nectar fit for the gods. When men drank a little of his wine, they sang like birds; when they drank a bit more, they thought they were strong as lions; if they drank too much, they acted like asses.

Heralded as the creator of wine, Bacco was crowned by his admirers with a coronet of grapevine leaves, studded with jewels of garnet grapes and emerald leaves.

Bacco actually is one of many green-growth allegorical figures collectively known as "Green Man." Green Man representations are considered to be archetypes of our oneness with the earth. Historians have ascertained that artists are prone to depict his persona in times of extreme ecological stress. The image of Green Man, in mythology and religion, has appeared worldwide throughout the ages carved in temples and cathedrals. Other variations of Green Man are the Green Knight of Arthurian Legends, Robin Hood, and Mother Earth or Green Woman.

While we mention a few
of the wine grape varieties,
there are over
5,000
in the world,
some dating back to the Roman Empire.
Scientists are currently using DNA "fingerprinting"
to trace the ancestry
of noble and common
wine grapes,
discovering some ignoble
liaisons along the way.

I am not a seer or teller of fortune who peers into cups to read tea leaves to call forth clairvoyance but simply an artist who has gathered hundreds of leaves in my portfolio; each one pressed, sketched or printed. Over the years, with the assistance of viticulturists and ampelographers, my leaf collection has been the source of great inspiration, from a creative and authentic standpoint, for wine-theme etchings, illustrations, wine bottle labels and papier-mâché masks.

The term ampelography comes from two Greek words: *ampelos* for vine and *graphe* for description. Chardonnay leaves, with only slightly indented sinuses, remind me of round, patinated, ancient coins – harbingers perhaps of the gold medals that may one day be reaped in wine competitions. Cabernet sauvignon leaves appear to be heralding their nobility by flaunting distinctive, Gothic-arched edges that are often bordered in scarlet hues and pierced with graceful apertures. I will be the first to admit that ascribing anthropomorphic qualities to grape leaves proves that my artistic license overshadows my scientific knowledge, but I can't help myself.

When we lived in Napa Valley, we rented a 100-year-old cottage located at the edge of beautiful Spottswoode Vineyard. The owners gave us permission to walk among the vines, sketch the many varieties of grapes, take photos and selectively pick a few leaves. For the four years that we lived in St. Helena, the thrill of waking each morning and looking directly up the vine rows to the Mayacamas Mountains never left us. In early spring we would watch for bud break and worry almost as much as the vineyard owners about frost damaging delicate buds. Late spring brought floraision, or flowering, of the would-be grapes, and late in summer, veraision – changing of the grape colors. All along the vineyard rows, the fuzzy, apricot-colored young leaf tips unfurled, turning into small yellow green leaves and eventually into verdant large leaves with their characteristic shapes.

Our wine grower friend Justin Meyer, former president of Silver Oak Cellars and author of *Plain Talk About Fine Wine*, describes the cabernet leaf as having "deep sinuses with a naked vein at the petiolar sinus." A petiole is the leaf stem, and the petiolar sinus is the space between the two lobes. When this opening is delineated by veins at the edge, the leaves are described as being "naked." Justin points out that the cabernet leaf is one of the few varieties, along with chardonnay, that has naked veins at the petiolar sinus. He ponders the question: "Is it only coincidence that the most sought after white and most desired red varieties have this common characteristic of identification?"

In hot climates modern viticulturists appreciate and encourage leaf canopies to protect grape clusters from sunburn. Conversely, in cool climates with less persistent sunshine, the canopy is manicured in such a way that the grapes are fully exposed to the elements of sunshine and breezes in order to promote ripening and prevent rot.

Long ago, leaves fascinated Leonardo da Vinci, who wrote, "Every shoot and every fruit benefits from its leaf, which serves as the mother giving water from the rain and moisture from the dew which falls at night from above and protects against the too-great-heat of the sun."

Throughout history, other artists have recognized the importance of leaves to life. Since ancient times recurrent images of anthropomorphic leaves in the persona of "Green Man" have appeared in sculptures, masks and paintings. Pagan foliate heads were carved in Roman temples, and even Bacchus, with his crown of grape leaves and clusters, is a variation of Green Man.

Green Man is classified by many art historians as an archetype expressing psychic photosynthesis. Christian leaf masks with foliated tendrils emanating from mouths and nostrils were sculpted between arches and on corbels in Gothic cathedrals throughout Europe and were portrayed by Renaissance artists Botticelli, Donatello and Michelangelo. English poet Samuel Taylor Coleridge described Green Man as one who "utters life through his mouth. His words are leaves." Grapevines have embellished crowns and gowns in real life, as well as in sculpture and painting.

Shuffling through my line drawings of grape leaves, I spot a large zinfandel leaf displaying its assertive character with deep lobes and definitively notched, Z-shaped teeth. A small pinot noir leaf, unlobed, floats over the zinfandel leaf; its narrow, lyre-shaped petiolar sinus and serrated edge contrast with the bold configurations of the zinfandel leaf. "Reading" these two leaves, I am reminded that while zinfandel's origins are still a bit murky, pinot noir, long a favorite of kings and clergy, can be traced back to the first century.

When I walk in vineyards with my sketchbook in hand, I enjoy being able to recognize specific grape varieties by looking closely at their leaves and focusing on their essence – ignoring any renegade leaves. For example, merlot leaves can be identified not only by their wedge-like shapes, but also by their club-shaped, lateral sinuses – often with an extra "tooth" appearing in that space.

Of course, immediate and positive identification can be achieved when winegrowers nail signs on their fence posts to name the varieties in the vine rows. I wonder if they do this for themselves or for us?

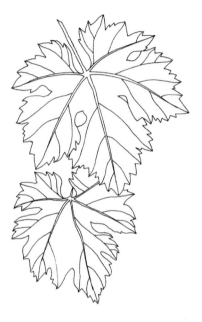

GRAPEVINE MENU

. . . .

FOGLIE RIPIENE

FILLED LEAVES

CHARDONNAY

SALMONE AFFUMICATO sopra TAGLIATELLE

SMOKED SALMON over NOODLES

PINOT NOIR

BISTECCA alla FUNGATA

STEAK with FRESH MUSHROOM SAUCE

CABERNET SAUVIGNON

SCHIACCIATA con l'UVA

SMASHED BREAD with MASHED GRAPES

PORT

FOGLIE RIPIENE

FILLED LEAVES

Selected for CHARDONNAY

8 servings

4 hard-boiled eggs, chopped finely

1 pint sour cream

1/2 cup sun-dried tomato bits

1 bunch chives, chopped finely

4 garlic cloves, chopped finely

2 teaspoons capers

1 teaspoon Dijon-style mustard

1 teaspoon pepper

1/4 cup Chardonnay

 Stir all ingredients together.

16 fresh endive leaves

 Spoon mixture into the endive leaves. Serve as an appetizer or salad.

SALMONE AFFUMICATO *sopra* TAGLIATELLE

SMOKED SALMON over NOODLES

Selected for PINOT NOIR

8 servings

PANNA PRIMAVERA – SPRINGTIME CREAM

1 can (19 ounces) New England clam chowder

1 can (10-3/4 ounces) cream of celery soup

1 cup white wine

1 pint heavy cream

2 garlic cloves, chopped

1 teaspoon coarsely ground pepper

1 ounce Amaretto

Chopped peel of 1 orange

4 teaspoons chopped basil

1/2 each red, yellow and green bell pepper, sliced in strips

8 artichoke hearts, chopped

> Mash clam chowder with potato masher in large bowl. Add cream of celery soup and wine; stir with wire whip. Stir in other ingredients.

8 handfuls of freshly made *Tagliatelle*

1 pound smoked salmon

1 cup grated Jack cheese

> Cook *Tagliatelle* in big pot of water, 1 minute. Drain *pasta;* add to *Panna Primavera*. Pour *pasta* and sauce in large baking pan and sprinkle small chunks of salmon over *pasta*. Cover pan with foil. Bake in 500-degree oven 20 minutes. Take the pan out; divide *pasta* among 8 plates; lightly sprinkle grated Jack cheese over each serving.

BISTECCA alla FUNGATA

STEAK with FRESH MUSHROOM SAUCE

Selected for CABERNET SAUVIGNON

8 servings

SALSA FUNGATA – MUSHROOM SAUCE

2 garlic cloves, chopped

1/2 cup olive oil

1/2 pound fresh mushrooms, cut into small pieces

1 cup heavy cream

Slowly sauté garlic in olive oil, add mushrooms and sauté over low heat for 15 minutes. Add cream and slowly simmer for 10 minutes, stirring occasionally. While grilling steaks, keep sauce warm in the top of a *bagnomaria* over hot water.

BISTECCA – STEAKS

8 filet mignon, all fat cut off

Pepper

8 spritzes of brandy

Sprinkle pepper generously over both sides of steaks and grill them over a very hot fire for 2 minutes. Turn steaks over, spritz some brandy over them and grill another 2 minutes. Pour *Salsa Fungata* over each *bistecca* and serve immediately.

This recipe is something I don't do every day because it requires a lot of attention and fast timing. It's also quite expensive, because filet mignon is the most expensive cut of meat you can buy. Especially with my theory of cutting off all of the fat from the meat, the cost increases 30% to 40%.

SCHIACCIATA con l'UVA

SMASHED BREAD with MASHED GRAPES

16 servings

Selected for PORT

L'UVA – MASHED GRAPES

1/4 pound "second harvest" red wine grapes – or market grapes

2 teaspoons fennel seeds

4 tablespoons honey

> Gently mash grapes and fennel and drizzle honey over. Cover bowl with a clean, white cloth and leave overnight.

SCHIACCIATA – SMASHED BREAD

1/3 amount of *Pane Campagnolo* dough recipe (page 58)

> The morning after mashing the grapes, prepare 1/3 the amount of dough described in the *Pane Campagnolo* recipe. With a rolling pin, roll out dough in a 14-inch circle to fit a 14-inch *pizza* pan. Bake in pre-heated 400-degree oven for 3 minutes. Remove from oven; turn *Schiacciata* over and spread grape mixture on top. With fingers, press grapes into dough. Bake at 350 degrees for 20 minutes. Allow to cool to room temperature; cut into 16 wedges; serve as dessert while celebrating the grape harvest!

The Italian word schiacciata means "smash," since the bread dough is smashed under the rolling pin. If you receive permission from a vineyard owner to pick some "second harvest" grapes (ones left over from the first harvest), ask if you can pick a few grape leaves. You will have the makings of a beautiful presentation by putting grape leaves around the Schiacciata making it look like a sculpture by Della Robbia. If using "bought" grapes from the market, you can decorate the plate with extra clusters of grapes instead of leaves.

Proud of his new vintage, winemaker Fortunato Sfortunati asked the two most respected wine tasters in town, Gargiano Gargiani and Luciano Lavacchini, for their enological evaluations.

"If I draw some of this liquid poetry from the barrel, will you please taste it and express your honest opinions? I will then have the honor to pass along your praises to the other *paesani*." Fortunato Sfortunati siphoned a sample of his precious wine into each of three glasses, and all three men held their glasses up to catch the light of the lantern to observe the color.

Gargiano Gargiani blinked at the brilliance of the color and pronounced, "Hmmm, this rich, ruby red hue portends excellence."

"*Si, si,* I agree," said Luciano Lavacchini.

Each man swirled the rich, ruby red wine in his glass to release the aromas.

Gargiano Gargiani tasted the rich, ruby red wine with the tip of his tongue. "My tongue is talking, but unfortunately you don't want to hear what it's saying. It tells me that this wine is flawed because it tastes like iron."

Fortunato Sfortunati raised his fist and his voice in anger upon hearing this unexpected critique. "How dare you disparage my beautiful wine! My barrels are sparkling clean and my wine is of the purest essence."

Fortunato Sfortunati turned away from Gargiano Gargiani and implored Luciano Lavacchini, "I'm sure that you will disagree with Gargiano Gargiani, thereby vindicating my vintage!"

Luciano Lavacchini skillfully swirled the wine once more and brought it toward his sensitive nose, sniffing. "Three sniffs are enough. My nose informs me that this wine is flawed because it smells like old Cordovan leather."

Beside himself with anger, Fortunato Sfortunati yelled, "Out, out, the both of you! Never darken my cellar door again, you charlatans."

After the wine in the barrel was bottled, Fortunato Sfortunati decided to scrub the barrel to ready it for the next vintage. To his chagrin, at the bottom of the barrel he found an old rusty iron key attached to a crackled Cordovan leather strap.

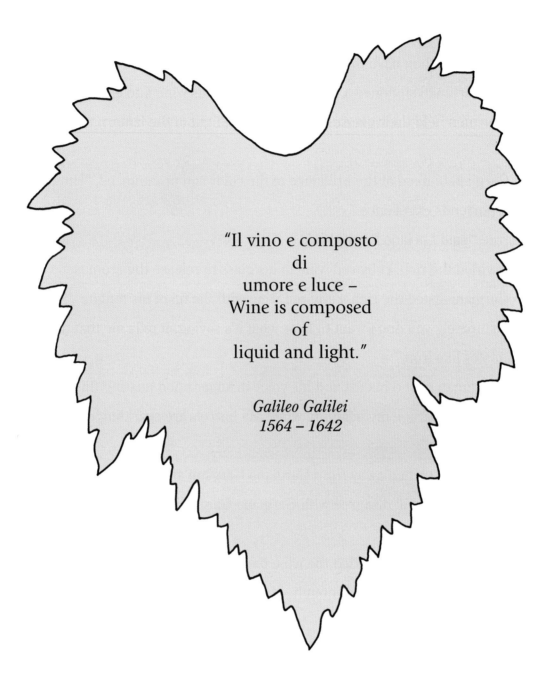

"Il vino e composto
di
umore e luce –
Wine is composed
of
liquid and light."

Galileo Galilei
1564 – 1642

Expert wine tasters have trained themselves to concentrate on their work, selecting nuances of the wine by blocking out any outside interference. They swirl wine in their glasses for two reasons: to check the appearance and also to create a slight evaporation thereby intensifying the aroma. In order to fully appreciate this aroma, they must first inhale sharply from deep within the glass, forcing the volatile esters to the olfactory organs at the base of the tongue.

Five criteria are crucial to wine tasting: The first aspect relates to the appearance of the wine, discerned by holding the glass to the light. The wine should be clear with the depth of color relating to the variety of wine. The second concerns the fragrance, both of the aroma of the grape itself and the bouquet that develops with the aging process. The third involves the taste, after sipping and rolling wine in the mouth to cover all of the taste buds. The fourth entails touch or mouth-feel. The fifth pertains to the aftertaste, which should be long-lasting, complex and pleasant.

Ruggero, who doesn't appreciate pretentious tasters, uses simple standards to judge wines, explaining, "First I look at the color, then I put my nose to work. After that, I carefully swirl some wine in my mouth and swallow a little bit. When I taste wine, right away I think about the food to go with it. In our *trattoria*, we have wines on our wine list that go well with our featured *pasta* and vegetables and with the small amount of beef, pork, chicken and fish that we serve. Even though I prefer red wine, I also taste whites and appreciate a few. I don't like over-oaked Chardonnays that take over the whole taste, because I want to taste the fruit, not the barrel. I like whites that are young and fruity, but appreciate Zinfandels and Cabernet Sauvignons that are three years or older. Pinot Noir and Sangiovese are okay younger. My thought is that a good meal is one that has wine with it, because the wine makes the food taste even better."

Ruggero calls my tasting method the "sixth sense" because I like to draw analogies from the wine, as illustrated by the following evaluation.

One day, glass of white wine in hand, I leafed through a lavishly colored art history book and came upon Sandro Botticelli's allegorical painting, "Primavera." A thought struck me about the use of "spring" in each work of art. "I'm tasting Primavera Mista white wine by Pedroncelli and looking at "Primavera" by Botticelli. Wondering if brothers John and Jim Pedroncelli, proprietors of the Pedroncelli Winery in Sonoma County, had indeed named their wine after the Botticelli oil painting, I phoned co-owner Jim Pedroncelli.

"That's an interesting thought," he replied, "but actually we just call the wine *Primavera Mista* because it reminds us of springtime here in the Dry Creek viticultural area and *mista* means mixed. This wine is our original white wine blend. We feel that the style is suggestive of the field-blended wines previously made by our father, John Pedroncelli. From this tradition, we've made our cellar-blend, using modern winemaking methods and oak aging. The best of each varietal is brought out, so that the sum is greater than the parts."

I looked again at the melange of figures portrayed in the Botticelli; an expectant madonna, graceful dancers, enticing angels and wary guards. All of the images, though contrapuntal, added up to a harmonious and total picture. Then Jim said, "We blend the distinctive wines in order to combine flavors artfully."

That did it! I swirled the wine in my glass, admired the pale gold colors, detected fresh fruit flavors, and took a sip. I could no longer resist expressing my analogy. "Jim," I insisted, "there is a similarity. The painting and the wine each have a central classic figure surrounded by a court of supporters. The Botticelli has a fruitful forest in the background, and the Pedroncelli has a fruitful vineyard in the background."

"Gina, I'd like to go along with you," he said. "But you see, we weren't even thinking about the famous painting. My brother John and I just wanted to make a white wine designed for a special niche, one that is associated with Italian foods. Our idea is that Primavera Mista will go especially well with *calamari*, *gamberetti* and *pasta primavera*." End of discussion!

Jim and John, with their Lombardy heritage and California experience, truly know and understand the nuances of Italian-style wine and food. John has been making wine since 1948, and Jim has been marketing those wines since the mid-1950s.

Their father, Giovanni "John" Pedroncelli, Sr., emigrated to the United States from Lombardia in the early part of this century. He worked on dairy farms and the railroad to save money to buy his own place. In 1927, his dream came true when he found a winery for sale in the hills overlooking Dry Creek Valley near the small town of Geyserville in Sonoma County, California. The terrain reminded Giovanni of his boyhood home, especially since the vineyards were planted in a field-blend. The winery had been established in 1904 but closed with the arrival of Prohibition. Giovanni maintained grape production by legally making 200 gallons of wine per year for the family and by selling grapes to home winemakers. After repeal, the winery produced bulk wines. Friends and neighbors carried jugs to the winery to be filled right on the spot, while San Francisco restaurants bought wine by the barrel.

The two sons worked right along with Giovanni. They've told me that they have fond memories of Silver, the last workhorse on the ranch. Mostly, Silver was used on the terraced hillsides as a "leaner."

"What does 'leaner' mean?" I asked Jim, thinking that I was going to learn a new agricultural term.

Jim chuckled, "Well, we leaned on Silver so that we wouldn't slip down the steep slope when we were working on the vines."

In the 1950s, Giovanni became one of the first northern Sonoma County vintners to bottle wines under his own label. Later he was one of the first to use the Sonoma County appellation. Though continuing to offer fatherly advice, Giovanni sold the winery to his sons in the 1960s. They began to produce single varietal wines and over the years they have received many awards for the quality and value of their wines.

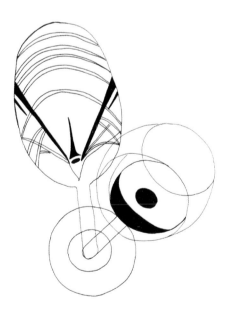

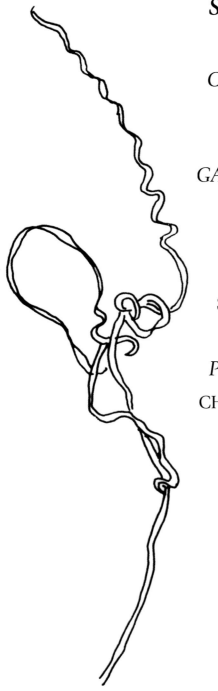

SPRINGTIME MENU
· · · · · · · · · · · · · · · · ·

CALAMARI ANTIPASTO
SQUID APPETIZER

GAMBERETTI ANTIPASTO
SHRIMP APPETIZER

PASTA PRIMAVERA
SPRINGTIME NOODLES

POLLO al VIN BIANCO
CHICKEN with WHITE WINE

FICHI con NOCI
FIGS with WALNUTS

CALAMARI ANTIPASTO

SQUID APPETIZER

8 servings

1 pound *calamari* – squid – (only the tentacles)

1/2 gallon water

> Place squid tentacles in a sieve and rinse in running cold water. Throw them in a big pot of boiling water. After water re-boils, turn heat down; simmer 5 minutes. Drain and rinse with cold water. Cut into 1-inch pieces.

Juice of 1 lemon

8 cloves garlic, chopped

1/2 cup olive oil

4 teaspoons vinegar

1/2 cup Italian parsley, chopped

2 teaspoons salt

> Drizzle lemon juice over cooled *calamari* in a bowl; stir in olive oil, vinegar and parsley; mix well and add salt. Divide into 8 portions. Serve with *Pane Campagnolo* and a young white wine.

Make sure that you follow this recipe by buying calamari tentacles. No other part of the calamari will do. This is a good antipasto for the spring, especially if you're having a picnic at the beach. You also could double this recipe and have it for supper with poco pane, poco vino – a little bread and a little wine.

GAMBERETTI ANTIPASTO

SHRIMP APPETIZER

8 servings

1 pound *gamberetti* – shrimp, cleaned, de-veined, pre-cooked

4 tablespoons olive oil

2 teaspoons pepper

4 garlic cloves, chopped finely

2 teaspoons Dijon-style mustard

> Rinse *gamberetti* and towel-dry. Cut each into 4 pieces and place them in a bowl; pour olive oil over. Stir to coat the shrimp with oil. Grind pepper over. Stir garlic into *gamberetti*; add mustard and stir again.

1/2 onion, chopped finely

1 fennel bulb, chopped coarsely

2 teaspoons capers

2 tablespoons vinegar

Juice of 1 lemon

> Add onion, fennel and capers. Pour vinegar and lemon juice over; stir well.

3 eggs, hard-boiled, peeled and chopped

2 tablespoons dry white wine

2 tablespoons sour cream

> Mash eggs with wine and stir into bowl along with sour cream. Refrigerate the covered mixture for at least 2 hours.

1 head *radicchio*

> Rinse, dry and separate *radicchio* leaves and arrange them in a circular pattern on a serving plate. Spoon some shrimp mixture onto each leaf.

PASTA PRIMAVERA

SPRINGTIME NOODLES
8 servings

SOFFRITO – SAUTÉ

1 cup olive oil

1/2 onion, sliced

1 sprig fresh rosemary, chopped

> Slowly sauté onions in olive oil until they are a light golden color; add rosemary and sauté 2 minutes more.

SALSA di PRIMAVERA – SPRINGTIME SAUCE

1 cup fresh mushrooms, chopped (the best in the market)

> Add to *Soffritto* and sauté 10 minutes, slowly

8 garlic cloves, chopped

4 ripe tomatoes, chopped

1/2 red bell pepper, sliced in strips

4 small *zucchini*, cut in half, then sliced lengthwise

4 carrots, cut in half, then sliced thinly lengthwise

4 small artichoke hearts, chopped coarsely

1/2 cup fresh string beans, cut in half

1 cup white wine

> Add these ingredients in this order and slowly simmer for 20 minutes. Pour *salsa* over freshly made and freshly cooked *Tagliatelle* – Noodles (page 41).

1/2 pound dry Jack cheese, grated

> Sprinkle cheese over each serving of *Pasta Primavera*.

POLLO al VIN BIANCO

CHICKEN with WHITE WINE

8 servings

4 de-boned, skinned chicken breasts

> Cut chicken breasts in half; trim off the thin end, skin and fat. With back of large knife, whack a grid pattern on both sides.

MARINATURA – MARINADE

4 eggs

Juice of 1 lemon

1 cup Sauvignon Blanc

2 teaspoons pepper

> Mix eggs in stainless steel bowl; stir in lemon juice, pepper and wine. Marinate chicken for 1 hour.

POLLO – CHICKEN

2 cups olive oil

2 cups flour

> Pour olive oil into large frying pan and bring to hot, but not smoking, point. Meanwhile, remove chicken from *marinatura* and dip each piece into flour, coating on both sides. Cook chicken pieces in hot oil, 4 minutes on each side. Set aside on warm platter.

SALSA al VINO BIANCO – WHITE WINE SAUCE

1 cup Sauvignon Blanc

1/4 cup Amaretto

> Turn heat off under frying pan; add wine and Amaretto, de-glazing pan by stirring liquid slowly with spatula and scraping browned chicken bits into sauce. Pour over chicken.

FICHI con NOCI

FIGS with WALNUTS

8 servings

8 black figs

Cut off tops and cut each fig in half horizontally

8 walnuts

> Shell nuts and break each one in half. Press each walnut-half into a fig-half.

8 ounces *Gorgonzola* or blue cheese

8 ounces dry Jack cheese

> Break cheeses into pieces and divide among 8 dessert plates, placing figs and walnuts in the middle of each plate.

I know that this fruit dessert is simple, and the question might be asked, "Do I really need a recipe?" I guess the answer is "Yes," because when you're having a Toscano meal, fruit and cheese often are just right for the finale.

Ruggero may cook Italian,
but he buys Californian:
Artichoke crowns from Pezzini in Castroville
Chestnuts from Genetti Ranch in Stockton
Dried fruit from Timbercrest in Geyserville
Dried *porcini* from Mendocino Mushrooms
Dry Jack cheese from Sonoma's Vella Cheese
Espresso coffee blends from Graffeo in San Rafael
Oil-cured olives and olive oil from Orland Olive Oil
and California wines:
Domaine Chandon
Groth
Meyer Family Port
Pedroncelli
Rombauer
Silver Oak

Friendly Farmer Vieri Vannini gave two sacks of his wheat grain to his neighbor on the north, Donatello Donatini. Pleased with such a fine gift, Donatello Donatini, in turn, gave Vieri Vannini six bottles of his green-gold olive oil. Vieri Vannini, excited by this neighborly exchange, took one sack of grain and three bottles of olive oil to Giampiero Giampieri, his neighbor to the south.

"*Grazie mille* – a thousand thanks," said Giampiero Giampieri as he led two scruffy donkeys out to the astonished Vieri Vannini. "I appreciate your generous gift so much that I am giving you my beloved donkeys, Argenta – Silver – and Mora – Blackberry. In time, you will understand just how valuable they are."

Disappointed to be burdened by the care of these two hungry and useless animals, Vieri Vannini managed to grumble a garbled "*Grazie,*" as he pulled and tugged at Argenta's rope and pushed and shoved Mora down the road. Upon finally reaching his home, his wife Graziella shouted, "Vieri Vannini! Are you out of your mind? What do you intend to do with those two miserable looking bags of bones?"

Vieri Vannini stuttered, "I don-don-don't have one clue, but I'll tie Argenta and Mora to the vineyard fence while we eat our supper and think about it." After eating Graziella's delicious *lasagne*, Vieri Vannini closed his eyes so that he could think more clearly about the Argenta and Mora problem.

The next morning, with no solution in sight, Vieri Vannini stumbled out by dawn's early light to give the donkeys some hay. He rubbed his eyes in disbelief because the two naughty donkeys had chewed through their ropes and disappeared. To his horror, he discovered that the two runaways had munched up and down his vine rows on their way to freedom and had stripped his grapevines of about 90% of their shoots. Vieri Vannini shook his fist and shouted an Italian vulgarity to no one in particular, "*Porca miseria* – Miserable swine!"

But at the end of summer when the farmer picked his grapes, he realized that his *vendemmia* – harvest – was the best ever. The donkeys' greedy but judicious pruning had greatly improved the quality of the grapes.

California Vineyards:
"Those lodes and pockets of earth,
more precious than the precious ores,
that yield inimitable fragrance and soft fire,
those virtuous Bonanzas
where the soil has sublimated
under sun and stars to something finer,
and the wine is bottled poetry . . . ."

Robert Louis Stevenson

1850-1894

Peering through the wavy-glassed window of our 100-year-old cottage in Napa Valley's St. Helena, I caught a glimpse of pickers silently slipping through early morning mist into the rows of grape-laden vines. Fog draped a filmy scrim over the tableau, creating a scene that could have been as ancient as the Roman Empire.

Fifty years before Christ, the Epicurean poet Titus Lucretius Carus had described a similar scene: "They tried to grow first one thing, then another on their loved lands, and saw wild plants turn tame in the soil with coddling and gentle, coaxing care. And with each day they made the woods shrink farther up-mountain, yielding room for farms below, for pastures, ponds and streams, grain-land, lush vineyards, their holdings on hill and plain, for olive groves to run their blue-grey bands like boundary lines flowing across the hummocks, dales and fields, as now you see lands everywhere picked out with beauty, lined and adorned with trees, and fruitful orchards wall them all about."

Lucretius' poetic words were as descriptive on this morning as they had been 2,000 years ago. Looking from our cottage across the vineyards belonging to Spottswoode estate, vine rows seemed to converge in vanishing point perspective. They were bordered by walnut trees in front, olive trees to the side and riparian shrubs at the far edge. Conifers studded the Mayacamas Mountain backdrop.

Sunshine began to stream through the clouds, spotlighting the workers. Voices were raised in Spanish cadence to match the rhythm of flashing knives skillfully cutting cabernet clusters. The pickers, with fingers and feet in fast motion, attacked four rows at a time, rushing with filled bins over their heads to the gondolas. Two gondolas were heaped with juicy blue-black berries by 8:30 a.m. As I gazed at the scene, dappled light played tricks with my eyes, turning perceived negative spaces into positive forms. I blinked a few times, flashing back to my favorite childhood coloring book activity. The line drawings were usually captioned with phrases like, "Find the hidden bears in the woods" or "Find the hidden hearts in the flowers." Taking my sketchbook out to the porch, I drew my own version: "Find the hidden workers in the vineyard." Several months after I had etched the elusive image of pickers within a canopy of cabernet sauvignon, I learned that the joke was on me. Not only were there hidden workers in that vineyard, but *invisible* workers!

These invisible workers had been employed since 1985 by vineyard manager Tony Soter upon the advice of viticultural consultant Richard Nagaoka, with the blessing of Spottswoode

Winery owner Mary Novak. Because her 46-acre estate and historic Victorian house is surrounded by homes on the west side of St. Helena, Novak wanted to be a good neighbor and avoid the negative aspects of spraying chemicals. Her workers actually are tiny wasps, so small that the human eye cannot see them. Officially titled Anagrus epos, their task is to control leafhoppers. The wasps over-winter on wild blackberries and consume about 90 percent of the grape leafhopper eggs. Subduing leafhoppers is desirable because the hoppers feed on grapevine leaf tissue, sucking out chlorophyll and causing mottled discolorations. Damaged leaves don't perform well in the photosynthesis process; also, excess defoliation exposes the grapes to sunburn.

Viticulturist Soter explained why the wasps were "hired."

"There was an opportunity to pursue the path of biological control. Besides my personal concerns about pesticides, I was worried about residues of the spray on the crop. Fortunately, we were in a situation that lent itself to natural control. The creek that borders the vineyard served as a habitat for blackberry bushes."

By encouraging these tiny wasps to work in the vineyard, only a small amount of defoliation occurs, just enough to thin the thick canopy of leaves and to provide optimum air circulation and sun exposure for the grapes.

Sitting on the front porch of our old cottage and daydreaming, I thought it just possible that the ancestors of our heroic wasp and villainous leafhopper may have been cast in similar dramatic roles during the time of Lucretius.

FARMERS MENU
· · · · · · · · · · · · · · ·

FRITTATA alle CIPOLLINE
OMELET with LITTLE ONIONS

LASAGNE al FORNO
LAYERED NOODLES in the OVEN

PERA e FORMAGGIO
PEAR and CHEESE

FRITTATA alle CIPOLLINE

OMELET with LITTLE ONIONS

8 servings

1 bundle fresh spinach

2 cloves garlic, chopped

4 tablespoons olive oil

5 green onions, cut into 1/4″ slices

16 eggs

Salt and pepper, to taste

1/2 cup dry Jack cheese, grated

Steam spinach for 5 minutes; drain in strainer, pressing down on spinach with a wooden spoon to "squeeze" out excess water. Chop spinach and set aside.

Sauté garlic very lightly in olive oil in skillet. Add spinach, mixing well; add onions and mix well; simmer slowly for 15 minutes.

Whip eggs in medium-sized bowl and then pour slowly over the ingredients in the skillet. Slowly simmer for 10 minutes, now and then sliding a narrow spatula under the *Frittata* in different places to help the liquid go underneath and cook. When everything looks finished, sprinkle the grated cheese over. Place skillet under the broiler flame for 2 minutes to melt cheese. If your green onions were picked in your garden, garnish with some of the purple blossoms just before serving.

LASAGNE al FORNO

LAYERED NOODLES in the OVEN

8 servings

16 cups *Sugo di Carne* (meat – page 130) or 16 cups *Sugo Ortolano* (vegetarian – page 180)

Recipe for *Tagliatelle* dough (page 41), fresh, uncut

1 tablespoon olive oil in one gallon of boiling water

4 cups grated dry Jack cheese

> Put a little *Sugo* in the bottom of 8 x 12 x 2-inch baking pan. Cut rolled-out *Tagliatelle* dough into five 8 x 12-inch rectangles. Drop one *lasagna* into large pot of boiling water. Take out as soon as it rises to the surface. Blot *lasagna* on towel; place it on top of sauce in baking pan. Pour 2 full ladles of *sugo* over *lasagna*. Sprinkle two handfuls of grated cheese, covering all of the sauce. Repeat these steps 4 times, so there are 5 layers of *lasagne*, ending with sauce and cheese. Cover pan with aluminum foil. Place in pre-heated 500-degree oven 45 minutes.

The reason this pasta is called Lasagne al Forno is because lasagne means wide noodles and forno means oven. If you wish to serve it later, you could put the lasagne in the refrigerator for a few days or in the freezer for a month tightly wrapped in plastic. I feel very secure when I have a pan of Lasagne ready, in case we want to invite some hungry friends at the last minute.

Actually, all of the pasta that I prepare in the trattoria is finished al forno – in the oven – because I have a very small kitchen and a lot of hungry customers. I can't be boiling water for every pasta order and making the whole trattoria steamy from big pots of boiling water. I "half-cook" my pasta in boiling water in the morning and finish cooking the pasta in the evening, after adding the appropriate sauce.

SUGO ORTOLANO

GARDENER'S SAUCE

8 servings

1/4 cup extra virgin olive oil and 1/2 stick butter

1/2 medium-sized red onion, chopped

1 twig rosemary, 2-inch-long, chopped

1/4 pound dried *porcini*, soaked in 4 cups hot water, drained, chopped

2 carrots, 10-inch-long, sliced crosswise, 1/4-inch thick

3 sticks celery, sliced crosswise, 1/4-inch thick

1 can (5-1/2 ounces) of tomato paste, mixed with 4 cans warm water

1 can (28-ounces) crushed tomatoes or 5 chopped fresh tomatoes

Juice and finely chopped peel of 1/2 lemon

4 garlic cloves, chopped

1/2 pound string beans, sliced in 1/2-inch lengths

2 *zucchini*, sliced crosswise, 1/4-inch thick

1/2 each of red, yellow and green bell peppers, chopped

1/2 cup peas

1/4 cup Mediterranean-style black olives, pitted, chopped

1-1/2 cups cooked *cannellini* beans, half whole beans, half mashed beans

Pinch red pepper flakes

> Lightly sauté onions in olive oil and butter in a large saucepan over medium low heat. Stir in the other ingredients. Simmer *Sugo di Ortolano* for 1/2 hour. Throw sauce over fresh hot *pasta*, or layer with *lasagne* and grated cheese for Vegetarian *Lasagne al Forno*, or use as *pizza* topping.

I like this sugo because it reminds me of my neighborhood ortolano – vegetable grower. Now I just go to farmers' markets.

PERA e FORMAGGIO

PEAR and CHEESE

8 servings

8 of the best pears of the season

1-1/2 pounds Jack cheese

Wash and dry pears. Cut each into fourths; peel and trim. Arrange around the edge of a serving plate. With the tip of a knife "break" the cheese into bite-sized chunks and heap in the middle of the plate. Pass the plate around the table.

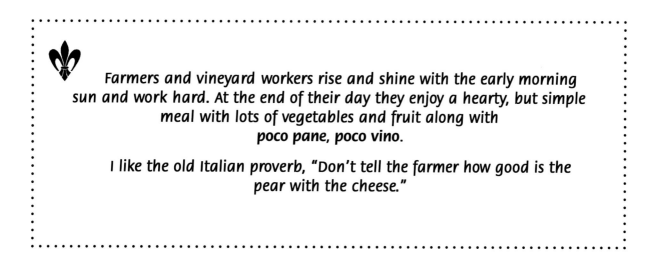

Farmers and vineyard workers rise and shine with the early morning sun and work hard. At the end of their day they enjoy a hearty, but simple meal with lots of vegetables and fruit along with
poco pane, poco vino.

I like the old Italian proverb, "Don't tell the farmer how good is the pear with the cheese."

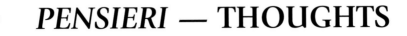

PENSIERI — THOUGHTS

When I was a very young man after the war, and I worked as a baker in the Forno Sartoni in Firenze, I often went to a little place. It was a **trattoria**, very down to earth. They didn't have too many choices, but they always had **pasta** and local wine. The wife was serving and the husband was cooking. There were paintings on the wall from hungry artists, who traded art for dinners. Sometimes a musician would come in and play violin or guitar, also in exchange for food.

In our **Villa Gigli Trattoria**, we keep the food simple and natural, with paintings on the walls and music softly playing, just like I remember in that **trattoria** in Firenze long ago.

Gina and I sincerely thank all of our friends and guests who come over the mountain to Markleeville to share **poco pane, poco vino** with us.

HISTORICAL FIGURES

Titus Lucretius Carus	98 - 55 B.C.E.
M. Gabius Apicius	80 B.C.E - 40 A.D.
Emperor Aulus Vitellius	15 - 69
Nerone Claudio Cesare	37 - 68
Dante Alighieri	1265 - 1321
Giotta di Bondone	1267 - 1337
Castruccio Castracani	1281 - 1328
Sandro Botticelli	1445 - 1510
Amerigo Vespucci	1451 - 1512
Cristofero Colombo	1451 - 1506
Leonardo da Vinci	1452 - 1519
Giovanni da Verrazzano	1485 - 1528
Giacomo Castelvetro	1546 - 1616
Galileo Galilei	1564 - 1642
Napoleone Bonaparte	1769 - 1821
Robert Louis Stevenson	1850 - 1894

FICTIONAL FIGURES

Astrancollo Astrancolli

Bianca Bandini

Berardo Beradi

Bruno Bruni

Corrado Carotti

Chino Chini

Cipriano Cipriani

Donatello Donatini

Dorina Dori

Fernanda Ferrini

Gargiano Gargiani

Giampiero Giampieri

Giovanni Giovannini

Giselda Giraldi

Lelio Landi

Lando Landini

Lucciano Lavacchini

Leoni Leoniero

Nicolo Nicolai

Paolo Panchetti

Pinucchio Panchetti

Piero Pierini

Renzo Rocci

Rolanda Romagnoli

Sergio Settisoldi

Fortunato Sfortunati

Siro Squilini

Tina Tucci

Vieri Vannini

These names were found in the census lists of old neighborhoods in the book *Caro Vecchio Borgo* by Aldo Giovannini, published in 1989 in Borgo San Lorenzo. As the former Jane Ellen Green, who became Gina Gigli through marriage, I especially admire their alliterative appellations. Though not acquainted with any of these mostly deceased Borghese, I have taken the liberty to "borrow" their charming names for fictional characters in *Poco Pane, Poco Vino*.

KITCHEN ITALIAN

aceto	vinegar	*cartoccio*	paper bag, parchment
acqua	water	*casa*	house
affumicato	smoked	*castagneto*	chestnut woods
aglio	garlic	*cenci*	rags
agnello	lamb	*cipolla*	onion
amfore	amphora	*cipolline*	little green onions
antipasto	appetizer	*colori*	colors
arrostire	to roast	*contadino*	farmer
arrosto	roasted	*convivio*	banquet
asparagi	asparagus	*coperta*	cover, topping
bagnomaria	double boiler	*coriandoli*	confetti
basilico	basil	*crema*	cream
bianco	white	*crostini*	toasts
bistecca	beef steak	*cuori di palma*	hearts of palm
bosco	forest	*diavolo*	devil
brodo	broth	*digestivo*	digestive
buon battuto	good chopped mixture	*dolce*	sweet
caccia	hunting or fishing catch	*duomo*	dome
cacciucco	fish soup	*espresso*	coffee
calamari	squid	*fagiolini*	small white beans
calderone	kettle	*farina*	flour
caldo	hot	*farina gialla*	cornmeal
calor	heat	*fegato*	liver
campagnolo	country	*festa*	festival
cannellini	small white beans	*festiva*	festive
cannelloni	filled pasta	*fettucini*	ribbons of noodles
cantina	wine cellar	*fettunta*	oiled bread slice
caratelli	wine barrels	*fichi*	figs
carciofi	artichokes	*fico*	fig
carne	meat	*filetto*	filet

KITCHEN ITALIAN continued

finale	finish	*macelleria*	meat market
fiori	flowers	*madre*	mother
focaccia	flat bread	*maiale*	pork
foglie	leaves	*malvasia*	white wine grape
formaggio	cheese	*mandarino*	tangerines
forno	oven	*mangiamo*	let's eat
forte	strong	*marina*	seashore
fragole	strawberry	*marinatura*	marinade
fredda	cold	*marrone*	chestnut
frittata	omelet	*mattone*	brick
fritti	fried	*mele*	apple
fungharella	mushroom sauce	*menta*	mint
funghi	mushrooms	*mescolone*	mixed
fuoco	fire	*miele*	honey
gallo	rooster	*migliacciole*	pancakes
gamberetti	small shrimp	*minestrone*	vegetable soup
giallo	yellow	*mista*	mixed
giardino	garden	*moscato*	white wine grape
gorgonzola	blue cheese	*mostarda*	fruit mustard
grazie	thank you	*mozzarella*	type of cheese
impasto	dough	*nebbiolo*	red wine grape
imperiale	imperial	*necci*	chestnut flour pancakes
insalata	salad	*nepitella*	catmint or thyme
intaglio	etching	*nero*	black
lagane	ancient Roman dried noodles	*noce moscata*	nutmeg
lasagne	layered noodles	*noci*	walnuts
latte	milk	*olio d'oliva*	olive oil
legno	wood	*olivo*	olive tree
coniglio	rabbit	*orto*	vegetable garden
luce	light	*ortolano*	market gardener

KITCHEN ITALIAN continued

paesani	country folk	*raccolta*	harvest
pancetta	Italian bacon	*radicchio*	chicory
pane	bread	*ramerino*	rosemary
panna	cream	*ricotta*	cottage cheese
parmigiano	white cheese from Parma	*ripieno*	filling or stuffing
pasta	noodles	*risotto*	cooked rice
pastasciutta	noodles with sauce	*rosa*	rosé
pepe	black pepper	*rosso*	red
peperoncino	hot pepper	*salata*	salted
peperoni	bell pepper	*salmone*	salmon
pesche	peaches	*salsa*	sauce
pesto	crushed, pounded	*salvare*	to cure
pignoli	pine nuts	*salvia*	sage
pinot bianco	white wine grape	*sangiovese*	red wine grape
pinot grigio	white wine grape	*scampi*	shrimp
piselli	peas	*schiacciata*	flat bread
pizza	flat bread	*secchi*	dried
poco	a little	*selvaggio*	wild
polenta	cornmeal mush	*semi di finocchi*	fennel seeds
pollo	chicken	*sgrafitto*	incised design
polpettone	meat loaf	*soffritto*	saute
pomarola	tomato sauce	*sorbetto*	sherbert
pomodoro	tomato	*sott'olio*	under oil
porcini	boletus mushrooms	*speciale*	special
porri	leeks	*spinacio*	spinach
prezzemelo	parsley	*spumoni*	fruited ice cream
primavera	spring	*spuntino*	snack
profumo	perfume, aroma	*stracotto*	overdone
prosciutto	air-dried, salted ham	*sugo*	sauce
quaglie	quail	*tagliatelle*	noodles

KITCHEN ITALIAN continued

taglierini	finely-cut noodles
taglieroni	widely-cut noodles
tartuffi	truffles
teglia	baking pan
torta	cake
tortellini	tiny twists of filled pasta
Toscano	Tuscany
trattoria	restaurant
trebbiano	white wine grape
tutti frutti	all fruit
umido	stew
umore	liquid
uova	eggs
uva	grapes
vendemmia	harvest
verde	green
verdure	vegetables
vignaiolo	grape grower
vin santo	dessert wine
vino	wine
vinsanteria	wine attic
vite	vine
vulcano	volcano
zucca	pumpkin
zuppa	soup

RECIPE BOX

ANTIPASTI—APPETIZERS

CALAMARI ANTIPASTO - SQUID APPETIZER 165
CROSTINI al FEGATINI - TOASTS with LIVER SPREAD 43
CROSTINI al PESTO - BASIL TOASTS 93
CROSTINI di TRE COLORI - TOASTS of THREE COLORS 128
FRITTATA alle CIPOLLINE - OMELET with LITTLE ONIONS 178
FRITTATA al FORNO - OVEN-BAKED OMELET 61
GAMBERETTI ANTIPASTO - SHRIMP APPETIZER 166
PROSCIUTTO alle NOCI - HAM with WALNUTS 83
UOVA alla DIAVOLO - DEVILED EGGS 44

CARNI—MEAT

AGNELLO ARROSTO - ROAST LAMB 63
BISTECCA alla FUNGATA - STEAK with FRESH MUSHROOM SAUCE 155
FILETTO con FICHI - FILET with FIG SAUCE 32
MAIALE al MIELE - HONEY-GLAZED PORK ROAST 46
POLPETTONE in TEGLIA - MEATLOAF in a PAN 129
STRACOTTO - "OVERDONE" ROAST BEEF 86

DOLCI—DESSERTS

BISCOTTI da VINO - TWICE-BAKED COOKIES for WINE 120
CENCI - RAGS (SWEET FRIED NOODLES) 76
FICHI con NOCI - FIGS with WALNUTS 169
FRAGOLE del BOSCO - WILD STRAWBERRIES 86
LATTE IMPERIALE - IMPERIAL CUSTARD 50
MELE al FORNO - BAKED APPLES 144
MIGLIACCIOLE - DESSERT PANCAKES 33
MOSTARDA - BERRY SAUCE 97
NECCI con COPERTA di CREMA - CHESTNUT FLOUR PANCAKES with
    COVER OF CREAM 132
PERA e FORMAGGIO - PEAR and CHEESE 181
PESCHE con VINO e MENTA - PEACHES with WINE and MINT 64
TUTTI FRUTTI - ALL FRUIT 109
SCHIACCIATA con l'UVA - SMASHED BREAD with MASHED GRAPES 156
SPUMONI - FRUITED FROZEN CREAM 96

INSALATE—SALADS

FOGLIE RIPIENO - FILLED LEAVES 153
INSALATA di CORIANDOLI - CONFETTI SALAD 141
INSALATA di CUORI di PALME - PALM HEART SALAD 31
INSALATA di POMODORI - TOMATO SALAD 106
INSALATA MISTA - MIXED GREEN SALAD 45
PASTA FREDDA con SALMONE AFFUMICATO - COLD NOODLES with
    SMOKED SALMON 107

RECIPE BOX continued

PANE—BREAD

CROSTINI al FEGATINI - TOASTS with LIVER SPREAD 43
CROSTINI al PESTO - BASIL TOASTS 93
FETTUNTA - OILED BREAD 59
FOCACCIA al RAMERINO - ROSEMARY FLAT BREAD 72
PANE CAMPAGNOLO - COUNTRY-STYLE BREAD 58
PIZZA MARGHERITA - QUEEN MARGARET'S FLAT BREAD 105
SCHIACCIATA con l'UVA - SMASHED BREAD with MASHED GRAPES 156

PASTE e POLENTA—NOODLES and CORNMEAL MUSH

CANNELLONI con CREMA ROSA - FILLED PASTA with ROSÉ SAUCE 61
LASAGNE al FORNO - LAYERED NOODLES in the OVEN 179
PASTA FREDDA con SALMONE AFFUMICATO - COLD NOODLES with
   SMOKED SALMON 107
PASTA PRIMAVERA - SPRINGTIME NOODLES 167
PASTASCIUTTA IN BIANCO - "DRY" NOODLES with WHITE SAUCE 75
POLENTA con PIGNOLI - CORNMEAL MUSH with PINE NUTS 142
TAGLIATELLE - BASIC NOODLES 41
TAGLIATELLE con SALSA di POMAROLA - NOODLES with TOMATO SAUCE 118
TAGLIERINI con SCAMPI al MANDARINO - NARROW NOODLES with
   TANGERINE SHRIMP 94
TAGLIERONI al POLPETTONE - WIDE NOODLES with MEATLOAF 131
TORTELLINI ala FUNGHARELLA - TINY TWISTS of FILLED PASTA with
   MUSHROOM SAUCE 84

PESCI—FISH

CACCIUCCO - FISH SOUP 95
CALAMARI ANTIPASTO - SQUID APPETIZER 165
GAMBERETTI ANTIPASTO - SHRIMP APPETIZER 166
PASTA FREDDA con SALMONE AFFUMICATO - COLD NOODLES with
   SMOKED SALMON 107
SALMONE AFFUMICATO sopra TAGLIATELLE - SMOKED SALMON
   over NOODLES 154
SCAMPI al MANDARINO - TANGERINE SHRIMP 94

POLLAME e SELVAGGINA—POULTRY and GAME

CONIGLIO al DOLCE FORTE - RABBIT with SWEET and SOUR SAUCE 143
POLLO al MATTONE - CHICKEN under BRICK 119
POLLO al VIN BIANCO - CHICKEN with WHITE WINE 168
QUAGLIE alla SALVIA - QUAIL with SAGE 60